The Funeral Parlor Quilt

a novel by
Ann Hazelwood

C&T PUBLISHING

"These books are addictive. Every time, the customer wants to know when her *next* book will be out!"

—Jim Erwin, Main Street Books, St. Louis, Missouri

"I am hooked on the Colebridge Community. I like the addition of Jean from England. Ann has so much compacted into each book. Love them and cannot wait for the next one."

—Joan Brown, St. Mary, Missouri

"The Colebridge Community comes alive through Ann Hazelwood's imagination with more adventures and mystery. It's a joy to watch her characters as they face life's challenges. The Colebridge Community series builds upon friendship and family. I'll be waiting to visit this little town soon!"

—Janet Lewien, Community and Children's Resources Board and member of the WEE WRITERS

"Ann Hazelwood captures the essence of family and friends in the unique community of Colebridge as she expands her tale and characters. We as "hometowners" smile as we find her books delightful to read, recognizing the similarities. The mysterious white lilies add a sense of intrigue. Always fresh, do they signify the purity and timeless devotion of true love? Just like our little flower shop in St. Charles, Missouri, Brown's Botanical is privileged to share in many of the happenings of the families whose life events are celebrated and acknowledged with flowers. What an honor and joy!"

—Holly Gillette, owner of Parkview Gardens and Nursery, St. Charles, Missouri

"Don't plan anything else when you start one of Ann's novels. There's nothing better than a good book, merlot, and chocolate."

—Sally Reardon, SalMar Quality Quilting LLC, St. Charles, Missouri

Text © 2013 by Ann Hazelwood
Artwork © 2013 by C&T Publishing, Inc.

Executive Book Editor: Elaine H. Brelsford
Copy Editor: Chrystal Abhalter
Proofreader: Joann Treece
Graphic Design: Lynda Smith
Cover Design: Michael Buckingham

Published by C&T Publishing, Inc., P.O. Box 1456, Lafayette, CA 94549

Library of Congress Control Number: 2013945322

Printed in the USA

10 9 8 7 6 5 4 3 2

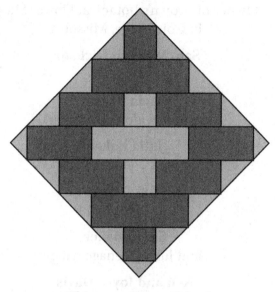

Chimney Sweep block

"I always thought of plants as little lives in a pot, just like books were like minds on a shelf."

CHARACTERS

Anne Brown
Owner of Brown's Botanical Flower Shop
in Colebridge, Missouri

Sam William Dickson
Anne's fiancé

Sylvia Brown
Anne's widowed mother

Julia Baker
Sylvia's younger sister

Jim Baker
Julia's husband

Sarah Baker
Jim and Julia's teenage daughter

Ken and Joyce Davis
Sylvia and Julia's brother and his wife; who live in Ohio

Sue Davis
Ken and Joyce's single daughter; who lives in Colebridge

Mia Marie Davis
Sue's newly adopted daughter

Muffin
Sue's dog

Helen and Joe Dickson
Sam's parents who live in the Chicago area

Pat and Elaine
Sam's sisters: Pat, a quilter, lives in Tulsa; Elaine lives in
Chicago

THE FUNERAL PARLOR QUILT

Ted Collins
Anne's former boyfriend

Sally
Flower shop employee; she is single

Kevin
Flower shop delivery man; he is single

Jean Martin
New flower shop employee from Bath, England

Al Martin
Jean's husband

Gayle
Shop owner of Gayle's Glass,
located next door to the flower shop

Donna Howard
Owner of Donna's Tea Room on Main Street

Richard and Nancy Barrister
Old friends who live in Boston

Abbey Kaufman
New employee of Brown's Botanical Flower Shop

Amanda and William Anderson
Half cousins

Mary Elizabeth Anderson
Half-sister to Sylvia, Julia, and Ken

Nora Newstead
Anne's housekeeper

With Appreciation

One does not fulfill one's creativity and success without the help and support of one's family and friends. I would like to acknowledge and thank the following:

First and utmost my heartfelt thanks go to my husband, Keith Hazelwood, and my sons, Joel and Jason Watkins, who continue to tell me how proud they are of my work. I love you!

My writer's group, The Wee Writers, especially Jan Lewien, who does early editing for me. Jan, Hallye, Lilah, Mary, Janet, and Ann are all very dear to me.

My friends Dellene, Bobbie, and especially Terry David, who's helped me out with her handiwork. Terry Gulickson and my sister-in-law Mary Hazelwood help me create outside the box with their ideas and humor.

Last, but certainly not least, is the C&T Publishing staff and Meredith Schroeder, who believed in this fiction series. I feel they are on this journey with me, and I hope to make them proud.

CHAPTER 1

S urprise!" the unexpected voices called.

"What in the world is going on?" I cried. "What are you all doing here? Is this not our Jane Austen meeting? Sam, what are you doing here for heaven's sake? Mother, help me out!"

"I'm so glad you're surprised, Anne," Mother said as she gave me a slight hug. "I have to admit that it was Jean's idea to surprise you with one more little pre-bridal party. To quote Jean, this is a really a 'bridal tea' for you, Anne!"

Sam, my fiancé, came to my rescue to give a kiss and hug of support. Jean Martin, an English employee at my flower shop, joined him in the excitement. I gathered this was to be a joyous occasion from the crowd's reaction, but I had not yet absorbed its reality.

"I took a shine to do this on my own, Miss Anne," she said with such excitement that I did not have the heart not to respond with a big smile. "Some of the street folks wanted to pop in on the fun, and I told myself that we may gain a few more members to our Jane Austen Club. So there it is in a jolly nutshell! We have scrummy biscuits and my favorite English tea, which you might fancy. It was no trouble at all. Your mum and Sally were most helpful."

Sally, my longest and most devoted employee at Brown's Botanical, would be of help as she knew most everyone on Main Street by name and which shop they owned. As I now looked about the room to see my guests, I noticed Sam was heading for the door. He blew me a kiss good-bye and made a motion to his ears like it was crazy noisy and he felt out of place.

My Aunt Julia and her teenaged daughter, Sarah, were the next to greet me. I wondered how her divorce from my Uncle Jim was proceeding. It was probably a real pain to have to deal with happy wedding details when her own marriage had fallen apart because of Uncle Jim's adultery with a woman he works with. My future husband, Sam, and he are best friends, plus they work together at the Martingale Company. Sam's handsome appearance and friendly manner could also be a threat to me in the future, I reminded myself.

I still couldn't believe how quickly we fell in love when Uncle Jim brought Sam to our Thanksgiving dinner. Sam had nowhere to go and my exit from my former boyfriend, Ted Collins, left the gate unlocked for a new relationship. Sam more than filled any space left open and I responded hard—hook, line, and sinker. The timing was perfect for him. He traveled a fair amount for the company and wanted to start putting down roots, as he often said.

We put down roots, all right. After I said yes to Sam's proposal of marriage, we purchased a large, run-down

Victorian house at 333 Lincoln in Colebridge. Sam found the abandoned house up on a hill, just waiting for love and attention. I was overwhelmed at the very thought of a house purchase that needed restoration because I already had my hands full at my flower shop, Brown's Botanical on Main Street in Colebridge. He didn't have to persuade me any longer with the purchase when I discovered the charming, glass-enclosed potting shed at the rear of the large house. My love for flowers and the mere thought of growing them from seed was always intriguing to me. The shaky, untidy, and overgrown shed would have been torn down by most folks, but not me. It was part of a dream coming true. Sam couldn't wait to use his handyman talents on the house renovation, and I immediately organized and planted as soon as I could make use of such a structure. Much of the work would be ready for our September wedding.

The gardens and grounds at 333 Lincoln were most impressive at one time. Albert and Marion Taylor, the previous owners of the estate, were quite interesting. Researching their history had become as important as the estate itself. Thanks to finding a crazy quilt hidden in the potting shed, we had learned the good, bad, and the ugly of Marion and Albert's lives. The papers used for the quilt's foundation revealed letters that my quilting friends and I had reassembled with amazing results.

"Anne, you are not going to believe who's here!" Mother said, taking my hand. "Follow me to the kitchen. It's a special surprise." I couldn't imagine what was next.

"Surprise again!" said Nancy Barrister, a longtime schoolmate who now lived in Boston. She held her arms open, waiting for my embrace.

"Nancy, oh my stars!" I said in total amazement. "You came all this way for my little bridal tea? You are crazy, girl! How are you?" I fell into her embrace with such gratitude. Our eyes glistened with unshed tears.

"I couldn't miss this, Anne," she said, laughing and crying at the same time. "I have to confess, however, that I was going to be here this weekend anyway, so I was delighted to hear there was this little party. It gets even better, Anne. Richard and I are moving back to Colebridge next month. I wanted to tell you in person."

"No way!" I shouted. Mother, too, looked shocked at the news.

"Richard agreed to take over the funeral home so his dad could retire," she went on to explain. "It was a big decision, but it was the right thing to do. We love Boston and hate leaving our friends, but then I thought of you, Main Street, and all the good times we had together over the years. I didn't want to e-mail you anything until I knew for sure. Now I'm glad I got to tell you in person. I think we're going to make an offer on a cute little house that's for sale on Jefferson Street close to the funeral home. We are trying to have a family, but so far it's not been in the cards as they say."

"Oh, how awesome, Nancy," I said in delight. "This is all too much news to take in! Did you get to meet Sam before he left?"

"Did I ever, girlfriend!" she replied, fanning her hands like she was hot. "What a hot hunk or catch or whatever you want to call him! He seems so different than Ted—or haven't you noticed that!" We both fell into deep laughter. Mother acted like she didn't hear her remarks. She had that same look on her face like when Nancy and I would get mischievous and silly.

"No kidding, Nancy, can you believe it?" I said, shaking my head in disbelief. "He is so wonderful. I didn't think I would ever meet anyone who would understand my commitment to the business, and he really does. He knows I don't cook because living with Mother, I never had to. He loves to cook, and he's been quite handy at our new, or should I say old, house! I know I've told you some things about it, but wait until you see it. I have my own potting shed, so how cool is that?"

"Yes, I remember your telling me about the quilt revealing a long lost relative," she remembered. "You'll have to fill me in on that. Richard drove me by the house, but we could hardly see any of it from the street. He said he was told growing up that the house was haunted. Did you scare the spooks away?" We laughed even more. Jean and others were now going in and out of the kitchen and letting us have our fun.

"I will fill you in on everything, Nancy. Did you meet everyone here?"

I made sure she did as we joined everyone in the living room. She already remembered Gayle from Gayle's Glass and Isabella from the quilt shop.

"Oh, I never miss going to Isabella's when we come to visit," said Nancy as we approached Isabella. "I am quilting more and more now, and I think she has one of the best quilt shops in the country, if you ask me."

"Oh, Nancy, you've made my day. So you will be living here in time for the wedding?"

"We will, indeed! I'm anxious for Richard to meet Sam before then if it's possible."

"We'll take care of that right away."

As Nancy started talking to Isabella, I joined the rest with a cup of tea. I greeted many shop owners I had been doing business with and even Mrs. Carter, who was our next door neighbor on Melrose Street, where I live with my widowed mother, Sylvia Brown.

Obviously missing was my cousin, Sue Davis, and her newly adopted daughter, Mia, from Honduras. Mother explained that Mia was ill and Sue did not want to leave her. Then I noticed there were no family members from the Dickson side of the family, such as Sam's mother or his two sisters, Pat and Elaine. The Dickson side of the family lived out of town so I assumed the trip was a bit much for a bridal tea after all. In the back of my mind, I wondered if the Browns and Dicksons would ever be a blended family. Was it too soon to worry about that? Hmmm...

CHAPTER 2

The next morning, I emerged downstairs in my sweatpants and oversized tee shirt to begin my morning walk. If Mother ever wanted a word with me before I started my day, I could count on her being perched with her newspaper and coffee at the kitchen counter.

"Did you ever connect with Sam after the tea?" Mother asked, still in her robe.

"Yes, that sneaky fiancé kept another secret from me," I lamented, shaking my head in disbelief. "I dropped some things off at 333 and he was still up putting books on his shelf in his study. I was anxious to find out why none of his family was at the tea."

"Oh, honey, I could have answered that. They were certainly invited, but I guess he told you how poorly his father is doing."

"Yes, I felt bad after I asked," I admitted, joining her with my mug of coffee. "He hasn't been the same since that last heart attack, and no one wants to leave him. Sam is going to visit as soon as he arranges some things at work. I sure wonder if Sam has inherited some of the weak heart genes."

"That's possible, Anne. He hasn't complained of chest pains again, has he?"

"No, not really," I said slowly, feeling my stomach churn. "He's not drinking as much and seems to be better about getting to the gym. He wants to someday have a workout room added to the garage. Maybe I can then remodel my potting shed. What do ya think about that?" Mother waved her hand at me like I was up to no good.

"I need to get in this walk. It looks like rain could come any minute! Nancy is still in town, so I'm going to try to meet her for lunch today. I'm so excited to have her here. Another generation of Barristers takes over the funeral home, which is so nice, don't you think?"

"Yes, I'm sure Richard's father is pleased. If they're going to purchase the cute little house that is for sale on Jefferson, it's the Thomas Keller home. It is the large yellow brick house with the two turrets and three floors. It's not so little and cute if you ask me. It must cost a pretty penny. The Kellers restored that quite nicely, I heard."

"Oh my. She did say it was a yellow brick. Maybe they are thinking of making it another funeral home!"

Mother laughed and opened the door for my exit.

"Good morning, you sneaky devils you," I called out to Sally and Jean who were busy working with bouquets when I arrived at the shop.

"It turned out quite swell, Miss Anne," Jean bragged. "Your street folks had a jolly good time, and that friend of yours, Nancy, is such a pretty thing and expresses all kindness in general."

"She called here about a half hour ago, by the way, and said she would call back," Sally spoke from the back room. "She said to tell you she was free for lunch and would check with you about what time."

"Will that work with what's on our plate today?" I asked Sally as I checked the computer. She always seemed to know the status of each order at any given time.

"Sure, we should be good Anne, but don't forget to add more dahlias to that warehouse order this morning or we won't have them in time for the Simpson funeral," Sally reminded me.

We continued our chitchat about the bridal tea until a customer came in, who I immediately responded to.

"Hi," she said when I approached her. "Is Sally here?"

"Oh, sure," I answered the unexpected question. "I'll go get her. She is working her fingers to the bone back here, but I'll manage to pull her away."

Sally looked puzzled when I told her someone was asking for her so she quickly washed her hands and went to the customer counter. Jean and I were a bit curious, so we stayed within hearing distance.

"Oh Paige," Sally greeted her in surprise, "what are you doing in the neighborhood?"

"Well, I thought I would check out where you work first of all, but I could also use another potted violet like the one you gave me. You have any?"

Sally looked puzzled and put her hands on her hips. "Sure, we keep some over here, where they get the perfect light," she muttered as she tried to help her.

Just then Gayle came in from next door to relate to everyone there that she had a really good time at the bridal tea. I came to the counter to thank her again for a lovely stained-glass vase that she made for me as a shower gift.

"I had never been to a real English tea before, Jean. It was very special," she bragged to Jean, who was taking it all in.

Out of the corner of my eye, I noticed Sally and her friend Paige whispering between themselves before they came to the counter to join us.

"Anne, this is my friend, Paige Beermann," Sally said directly to me.

"Nice to meet you, Paige," I said cheerfully. "That is Jean over there piercing the roses and this is Gayle from Gayle's Glass next door."

"Yeah, I've heard of you all," she responded. She smiled from ear to ear.

"You'll love that variety of violet you're purchasing," I shared. "They need a north window if possible, but they are the heartiest of all."

"Say, Miss Paige," Jean chimed into the conversation area, "you aren't a Jane Austen fan are you?" Paige gave a puzzled look. "Did Sally tell you about our little book club? We're trying to get a few more members if you'd like to come with Sally. We have a jolly good time and a spot of good English tea to boot!"

"No, that would not be for Paige, Jean," Sally quickly responded for her friend.

"I'll have you know, Miss Sally Know-It-All, I have read her book *Emma* and enjoyed it very much, actually. The moral of the story is we should try to improve our own character and not interfere in other people's lives." Sally was stricken by her comment, and we waited silently for the next remark.

"Well done, my lady," said Jean perking up. "I'd say you qualify most nicely if you'd like to visit."

Paige gave Sally a snickered look, paid for her purchase, and left. I felt there was something more to this visit than someone needing another violet for her collection. Sally went quietly to the design room and continued her arrangement in progress.

Nancy called to confirm a late lunch date and I was more than happy to leave an uncomfortable cloud of tension between Jean and Sally.

CHAPTER 3

I asked Donna Howard, the owner of Donna's Tea Room, to give us a quiet table in the corner so we could visit without being interrupted. Donna, a longtime resident of Colebridge, knew Richard's side of the family and was pleased to meet Nancy. Donna's place had the Victorian charm and warmth that so many looked forward to—not to mention the delicious food.

"I have so many things to talk to you about, Anne," Nancy eagerly confessed. "Having personal conversations in e-mail is just not my style, I don't know about you!"

"You're happy about the move here, aren't you?" I asked, wanting to get that out of the way first of all.

"Oh, I think for the most part," she slowly responded. "It will be good for us career wise for sure. Richard is concerned about whether his father will really let him take charge like he hopes to. What I am most unhappy about, Anne, is our inability to have a child. Richard won't seek professional help on the matter. You know how private some men can be. He just thinks it will happen in time. In my opinion, he's just too busy to want to think about it and doesn't want anything to crowd our lifestyle."

"I can't believe that's true," I challenged, trying to give Richard a break. "You know, he may be right that this change of lifestyle here in Colebridge may get your mind off of it and then nature can take its course."

"Well, we'll find out I suppose," she said sadly. "I'll be very busy redoing some things in that house, that's for sure. I'll be counting on you for some references, since you and Sam seem to be renovating. Some of the gaudy colors will not do, and I want to update one of the bathrooms. I can't wait to see this 333 Lincoln home you'll be living in. You've got to be so excited!"

"Sam is sure loving it," I said, shaking my head in disbelief. "He moved in last month. I hope he'll still want me to join him." Nancy laughed. "I go there every day moving things from home I don't need. I think Mother is trying to clean house at the same time and thinking everything should now go to Lincoln Street." Nancy agreed with the thought as she snickered.

"She will really miss you, won't she?" Nancy said smiling. "You may actually miss your home more than you think. You haven't lived anywhere else, have you?"

"Going to community college helped me save money and then after my dad died, I just couldn't leave Mother. I have to admit that she made it too easy for me to stay. Ted was always trying to convince me to move into my own apartment, but he wasn't convincing enough."

"He wasn't very convincing on anything with you, was he?" Nancy quipped.

"Not really," I answered somewhat sadly. "Hey, I'm curious. Are you are going to work part time at the funeral home like you did in Boston?"

"That's our plan, but I don't know for sure what the atmosphere will be with his father coming around in his retirement." She began studying the menu. "Women didn't work much in his day and time in the industry, unless it was in the office. I don't know how he will take to me coming and going. Richard said not to worry about it."

"Just get the turkey melt with her house salad and you'll be more than pleased," I suggested as Nancy pondered. "It's what I get all the time, unless her soup of the day tempts me. The real treat comes when Donna comes over and offers us a complimentary piece of coconut cream pie. It is to die for and she's known nationwide for it. The pie crust has to be pure lard, it's so yummy!" Nancy's eyes perked up.

"Fine by me," she said, rubbing her hands together. "If I can't get fat with a baby, I'll just enjoy all this delicious food in Colebridge."

We both laughed again and it felt so good to have her company. I now was beginning to realize how much I missed having a close friend around. I felt my friendship was limited with my employees, as much I thought of them.

"Anne, may I be so bold as to invite myself to your little quilting group that meets in your basement?" She gave me a shy smile. "I no doubt will enjoy your little Jane Austen group, but I'm really into this quilting. I made a really special quilt for our funeral home in Boston, and it gave me such satisfaction to see people's reactions."

"Wait just a minute, Nancy—I'm not sure I understand," I responded, reacting in surprise. "You made a quilt for the funeral home?" The look on her face let me know she had introduced a subject of unknown territory with me.

"I did," she confirmed. "It isn't a new idea. I have studied how quilts were used in the funeral and burial process in different cultures and religions. In the Victorian era, for example, some funeral homes would have a fancy, decorative quilt on hand to lie on top of the casket or sometimes inside the casket. These kinds of quilts were made for homes as well, when they laid out their family members on couches or doors that were removed for the occasion. They wanted something special, as you can imagine. They were usually made out of silks, velvets, satins, ribbons, and tons of fancy embellishments." I paused to picture it.

"My word, did they by chance look like a crazy quilt?"

"What's this?" Nancy now looked surprised. "You know what a crazy quilt is?"

"Yes," I responded between the delicious bites of my salad. "That was the pattern of the quilt I found in my potting shed. Remember the quilt with the cut-up letters attached I told you about?" She did not respond with her mouth full. "Well, it had no backing other than those papers attached to each piece. Jean said promptly that it was not that uncommon to find crazy quilts unfinished."

"My word, this is all quite tasty, just like you said, Anne," Nancy said, taking another bite of the sandwich.

"Well, I can't wait to see it. The one I made for them to use was more like a friendship quilt design so that names could be signed in the plain squares. I also made it out of satins, silks, taffetas, velvets, and various ribbons to make it look Victorian. I'll never do that again. The fabrics were very difficult to work with. The response from families was generally quite positive when we told them they could use it at the funeral. Some wanted no part of it. Some quilters who passed had their own family quilts to display, which we encouraged, of course. The home in Boston wants to keep the one I made so I want to make one for this place, especially since it will be in Richard's family's funeral home."

"No doubt our quilters will want to hear all about this and perhaps be helpful in some way," I added. Frankly, I wasn't really sure what they really might think. Leave it to my creative friend Nancy!

"That would be great because I have an idea I'd like to explore with them," she announced as she got more excited. "Of course, I want to run it by Isabella as well. It will be such fun having Isabella's at my fingertips. When will you meet again and what are you quilting these days?"

"It's my Botanical Beauty flower quilt that Mother made for me." I smiled proudly at the picture of it in my mind. "She thinks it has to be my wedding quilt, but I know just where I want to hang it in my shop. It's all flowers, of course, so it will be perfect there. It took her forever to hand appliqué all those darn pieces."

"Wow, are you lucky or what?" she envied. "I can't wait to see it, and I would be honored to quilt some stitches on it. Please let me know when you meet again. I knew things would work out coming back. Oh, I can't wait."

We did, indeed, have much to catch up on and our lunch lingered longer than it should have. It was going to be fun having a friend to call my own who knew me so well from the past. There were always so many differences between us, but it never mattered with our friendship. I was certain that having Nancy and Richard here would not only be a great addition for Colebridge, but also in the lives of Anne and Sam Dickson.

CHAPTER 4

Sam called to tell me he was leaving later that day to see his father. Instead of my usual walk, I decided to go by his house to say good-bye. He had so much on his mind, just as I did. When I arrived, I walked right in and found he was still packing in his upstairs bedroom.

"Glad you woke up in time to see me, Annie," he quipped, greeting me with a hug. I loved it when he called me Annie. "I haven't been very attentive lately, but I am very worried that my father will not make it to our wedding."

"Hey, I understand." I hugged him back sympathetically. "I've been praying for him and your entire family. What can I do here while you are gone?"

"You can check around the grounds and continue to get as much of your things here where you belong," he ordered, still embracing me. "It's been dry these days, so until we get some kind of sprinkler system, you may have to take charge of the watering."

"Yes I know. The potting shed is like a heated oven." I was now sitting on the bed as he continued to pack. "I'm going to water before I leave this morning. The herbs love this weather, but some of my flowers are looking sad. I'm hoping when you return we can have dinner with Richard and Nancy. It will be such fun having them here. She is going to join us for quilting on Sunday afternoon. I wish we would have had her expertise some time ago." Sam was not paying attention to my chatter as he went back and forth from his dresser to the bathroom.

"I can't tell you my return date," he mumbled. "Mother has so many details she needs help with and I feel guilty that my sisters have had to do everything. I hate being away from you, sweetie." He now sat next to me and turned my face toward him. "Always remember, no matter where I am, I love you more than anything, and how much I am looking forward to September 12. You haven't mentioned much about the wedding lately. Is everything under control?"

"Sam, remember I have a mother who hasn't let me forget any detail," I shared with a laugh. "I am pleased she is enjoying the process because it could be the other way around. Actually, we are in great shape. I have my last fitting on my dress tomorrow and hopefully that won't change. I hope you'll love it when you first see me coming down the aisle."

"I'll love removing the gown even more," he teased as he kissed me again.

"Are you watching your time?" I queried, glancing at the clock on the bedside table.

"Yikes! I am out of here!" He picked up the bag to go

down the stairs. "Oh, would you turn off the coffee pot? I'll call you tonight."

"Love to all the family, Sam," I called as he went down the stairs and out the door.

He waved good-bye from the car, throwing me a kiss. Please keep him safe, I prayed. I didn't want this gift from God to ever go away.

As I tidied up and drank the last of the coffee, I walked around the spacious house noticing how well Sam's furniture had found its place, just like he planned it all. His oriental rugs were perfect in just the right places. His neatness was obvious, just as I noticed at his loft on the riverfront. The house was even becoming part of my world as well, as I saw some of my art on the wall and accessory pieces I had already delivered from home. My bedroom furniture would be going in one of the guest rooms after my last night on Melrose Street. I had already claimed most of the big closets. So far, Sam had not voiced any opposition.

I then remembered my watering duties and how my morning hours were disappearing. I locked up the house and proceeded to my potting shed. It was like a humid bath-house in which I could hardly breathe. Still hanging were the brand new gardening tools that mysteriously appeared from my ghostly Grandmother Davis. She had been respectfully calmer since our pleasant reunion with her daughter Mary, who she had to give up for adoption. Albert Taylor, who once owned these grounds, had cast my grandmother aside when she became pregnant with Mary in their little affair. When I found the paper-pieced quilt under the counter in my potting shed, it had revealed cut-up letters telling the story. She has to rest easier now that the mystery was solved and her daughter Mary and her children are part of our family. I feel her good blessing on Sam and me as the new occupants of 333 Lincoln, even though her ghostly spirit here is known all over town. People want to warn me about our ghost when they learn that I will be living up on the hill. So far, her activity has only consisted of flashing lights and gifts that have no explanation. Sam and I decided we could easily live with that. I had talked to her on many occasions, and will continue to do so when called upon. I will someday write a book about Grandmother Davis, and somehow I know she will be most helpful. Would she continue to show her spirit in the basement at my mother's house? That was the bigger question. When do spirits move on exactly? Hmmm...

CHAPTER 5

✻⌇✻

Sam's phone calls from his home were depressing and his father's health was not improving. What if he were to die right before our wedding? Sam already made it clear we would have to wait and see about any honeymoon plans because of his health. Tonight was Saturday night without my Sam. Mother was delighted as we spent the night packing things and eating Pete's Pizza. I was going through books and deciding which ones to take. Mother thought she'd just keep her favorites and then we could donate the rest to the book fair at the library. Each book had its own memory: when I read it, who gave it to me, or when I purchased it. I was careful to keep my Jane Austen classics in case anyone in our group hadn't read one or two. It turned out to be a nice evening of quality time with Mother. It also gave us some time to catch up on wedding details. I was certainly pleased that the event wasn't any bigger than planned and would be happy when it was all said and done.

"I'm dead tired, Anne," Mother announced at eleven o'clock. "This is past my bedtime, and I want to get up early to make a Boston cream pie for tomorrow afternoon. I don't even know if I'll make it to church."

"I'm right behind you as soon as I fill this box." I worked faster. "I'm going to take a nice soak in the tub tonight and make a list of things that keep popping in my head. Sleep well, Mommy dearest." I blew her a kiss.

The soaking did me good. I used to take time to indulge in such a manner, but quick showers were now usually in order each day to save time. For a quick moment, I pictured the oversize tub in our new bathroom at 333 Lincoln. Putting on my thick white robe instead of my nearly shredded chenille one, I nestled in bed and reached for my journal. There were always so many topics that juggled in my mind on what to write about, but tonight my thoughts were only on Sam. I shall write a little poem, I thought to myself.

Sam is more than half of me;
He is what makes me whole.
Without his love that I contain,
My body lacks a soul.

As I let the pen and journal fall, I fell into slumber envisioning a billowy cloud on top of a hill. I was greeted by a white vision of Grandmother Davis, who then introduced Sam to me. As I started to grasp his hand he faded away, which left me heartbroken. Then white visions of my friend Nancy came to me and said, "Let me take him...let me take him." It made me come awake with a slight whimper.

The next morning, I tried to recall what I knew was a sad dream, but it had gone. The sun was shining in my window and it reminded me of a quilting day with dear friends and family. I smiled at the thought and smelled the coffee brewing in the downstairs kitchen. A good walk along the river with a quick stop at the shop to check on a few things would be in order and then back to the Botanical Beauty quilt that awaited us all in the basement.

CHAPTER 6

I was pleased coming home from a good walk and finding an encouraging e-mail from the Good Shepherd Church, wanting us to do their altar flowers each month. How we had achieved this job was beyond me, but it was good news for a really tight budget. The day went quickly and I was excited about everyone coming to quilt tonight.

"Glad you're home, Anne," Mother greeted. "I haven't been in the basement to straighten up, so could you do that before you shower? That Ellie Carter called this morning and kept me way too long on the phone. I think she was fishing to find out if they would be invited to the wedding. I know your list is limited so I dared not make any comments."

I laughed, running downstairs to turn on proper lighting for the quilting and to make sure we had enough chairs around the quilt frame. To my surprise, we did. I guess Grandmother already knew Nancy Barrister would be joining us. The tray of thimbles was placed on top of the quilt, which was strange because we all had our thimbles and hadn't gotten out Aunt Marie's thimble tray since Sarah had joined us for quilting. I left it in place in case Mother was thinking ahead that Nancy might not have a thimble.

Oh my, my, this basement had memories. I remember sitting here crying the night I broke up with Ted and getting make-up on our quilt as I fell asleep. The next morning, to my delight, it had all disappeared. Thank goodness the spirit of Grandmother Davis seemed to be on my side of things.

Having gone upstairs to get ready, I was barely dressed when I heard voices entering downstairs, and it dawned on me that I was so busy I hadn't eaten a bite of lunch. Perhaps I could sneak a bite before I joined them in the basement.

Everyone gathered in the kitchen until we were all in attendance. Nancy was the last to arrive, which didn't surprise me. She had met everyone at the bridal tea so it was an easy re-introduction. Sue carried in Mia, who was sound asleep with her nap, so she went directly downstairs to make her a pallet on the floor in the corner of the basement. I was glad to see they had left Muffin, their dog, at home. He could become a real distraction sometimes.

"Oh, Mrs. Brown, I have such fond memories of your home," recalled Nancy. "I had many a sleepover here and we usually ended up going in the basement, Anne, remember?"

"Oh, indeed," I answered with a silly laugh. "We didn't want anyone to hear us and we were pretty convinced my bedroom next door to my parents was too dangerous." They all laughed and commented about some of their memories coming over to my house when they were all younger.

"I have coffee, tea, and wine downstairs and a nice treat

for you all later," announced Mother as she led them down the stairs. "Jean, I remember having these little tea cakes at the bridal tea. Thanks so much for bringing these."

Sarah stayed in the kitchen to finish talking on her cell phone. I grabbed a piece of turkey out of the refrigerator to satisfy my immediate hunger and held my finger over my lips to send a message to Sarah to be quiet about it. She giggled, hung up, and we joined the others.

"That was a nice gesture to get out the thimbles, Anne, in case Nancy needed one," Mother said with a grin. "But Nancy, I see you brought your own! It's quite beautiful and an antique, right?"

"Wow, Nancy, was that in your family?" I asked, looking at it closer. Before she could answer, I said, "Just so you all know, I didn't put the thimble tray on the quilt. I knew with all the quilting Nancy does that she would have her own."

"Well, Nancy, our grandmother was just looking out for you like she has done for the rest of us," teased Aunt Julia.

"Grandmother?" asked Nancy with a puzzled look. "I was just about to tell you it was MY grandmother's thimble so that was nearly correct!" We all joked about the coincidence and Nancy just knew enough to know we had strange occurrences in our basement and didn't pursue the explanation.

"Well, it's very beautiful, Nancy," I said as I passed around the thread for everyone to cut and thread their needles. "I told the others you would fill us in on your funeral quilt that you're making for your family's funeral home."

"A quilt for dead people?" Sarah joked right away.

"Sarah, for heaven's sake, let her talk," scolded Aunt Julia.

The basement got very quiet as we threaded our needles and listened to the description of the quilt that Nancy was making, and how they had used a funeral quilt at the funeral home in Boston. She thought the design worked nicely because of the strip in the middle to sign the family name. I watched the reaction of everyone's face as she emotionally described families' reactions when there was a homemade quilt to provide a human touch to the deceased. No one quilted until she took a pause.

"I think it's wonderful, Nancy," said Sue, who was the first to respond. "So, some take the quilt with them when they are buried?"

"They did more so years ago, according to history," she explained. "Think about the babies and folks dying as they went across the prairie. They couldn't just put them in the cold ground without wrapping them in something. The diaries of the 1800s tell of such circumstances, especially for the babies. Think about the times during the Civil War. Not only were soldiers buried in their quilts, but folks wrapped and buried their silver and precious belongings in quilts to hide them from the soldiers."

"It's very calming to the spirit, I suppose," said Jean in her sweet British voice. "My share of this conversation is to tell you that in England we have no such practice, however, a shroud of sorts is sometimes used. This is a lovely bit of knowledge I find quite intriguing."

"Oh yes, Jean," Nancy continued. "Shrouds are still referred to in many religions. Some keep a white shroud that they use for each funeral held at their church. It is to signify that we are all one. No one is better than the other. If you find tombstones interesting like I do, notice how many shrouds there are carved in stone. They have fringe and tassels like any textile, all very lifelike. It makes you want to touch them."

"This is all too creepy for me," said Sarah as she got up to go get a Coke out of the downstairs refrigerator.

"Well, Nancy, this is all fascinating stuff but how about we take a coffee break," Mother suggested.

"I'm sorry, you guys. We aren't getting much quilting done, are we?" Nancy said in jest.

"That's nothing new down here," I joked. "We'll have this quilt done in no time. When we quilted Mia's baby quilt, which was about this size, we were done in two or three weeks."

Down the stairs came the Boston cream pie and plate full of Jean's small tea cakes. Since Jean was now attending our quilting, Mother brewed special tea for her. When Jean told Mother that the queen never used a tea bag in her life, Mother thought it should be so in this house as well, for she enjoyed a good cup of tea herself. Milk always goes in first, Jean would remind us, when having tea at her house.

By now, Mia heard us stir and came crying to her mother. She would have no part of the hugs and kisses from others who wanted to get their hands on her. It was a wonderful scene to see Sue with the beginnings of her own family. I only wish she could find a nice man someday who would care for her and Mia.

Making side chatter before we sat down to quilt, Jean asked, "The Miss Paige Beerman we met last week, is she a close friend of Sally?"

"I really can't tell you, Jean," I answered. "It's the first time I've met any friend of hers. I was glad to meet her. Sally is such a private person. She never mentions family. She came to have Thanksgiving with us because she had nowhere to go. I hinted once if she had a boyfriend, and she quickly reminded me she had no time after going to school and working part-time. She is so dedicated to me and the shop, I never had reason to pry."

"She's just very quiet," offered Sue. "She's a great designer, Anne. You need to hang onto her."

"Oh, indeed," chimed in Jean.

"I know how lucky I am," I responded without making any more stitches. "I'm sure, in time, we'll all know more about her personally. I know I could leave the shop anytime and she'd know exactly what to do and when. I really need that kind of help as we grow."

"I wish I could give you more time at the shop, Anne," claimed Sue. "Mia has certainly changed my life. I rush home every day to spend any extra time with her. There are times I feel so guilty about taking responsibility for her and then leaving her so much. Maybe when she's older I can help you more."

"You're doing all the right things," added Mother. "There's a time and place for everything and now is the time when you need to give Mia what she needs. You have been a very good mother."

"I'm envious of you, Sue," said Nancy with a sad look on her face. "You know how much I want a child. Unfortunately at this point, Richard wants to wait and see if I become pregnant, instead of pursuing adoption. I admire the step you took, all on your own!"

We had all stopped quilting as we shared the serious conversation. Would I ever feel like Nancy and Sue and wish for a baby Dickson? Somehow the mere thought was nothing I could comprehend. Hmmm...

CHAPTER 7

Weall gave our quilting another try, except for Sarah who was entertaining Mia. They both had short attention spans, and it was actually helpful to us to have them play together.

"I would like to share an idea I have with all of you if you don't mind giving me your honest opinion," said Nancy, who was now feeling comfortable with our little group. "I want to repeat a funeral gesture that was done in the Victorian era. When a baby died, which was quite frequently, the funeral home would have available a small satin or silk quilt for the baby. They had a pink one for girls and a blue one for boys. It was an optional quilt that the parents could bury their baby in or they could just use it for display when the casket was open. If the quilt were removed at the close of the casket, they would then present the quilt in a little matching box. The original antique one I saw had the word Baby in the lid of the box, with sweet fancy ribbons and such. No one is ever prepared when a baby dies, like they are with an adult, so it's such a nice touch, don't you think?"

"Oh my word, Nancy, that is a precious idea," said Sue almost in tears. "I can just see the scenario of that presentation, and what a keepsake!"

"Especially for premature babies," Nancy quickly responded. "That's still their baby, and parents want some sort of a funeral despite the age of the child."

"So you want to know if it's a good idea?" asked Aunt Julia.

"Well, I'm convinced it is," stated Nancy. "I could possibly find something at the expo next time I go, but I am thinking these little quilts, which are quite small, should be handmade with loving hands. The antique one I saw was tied with tiny ribbon instead of quilted. I could find boxes at the expo to coordinate with them, I think, but I also was thinking that a satin envelope with a ribbon would suffice as well. We go to New Orleans next month."

"An expo, Miss Nancy?" asked Jean. "What is an expo and where does one find one of those?" We all had to laugh, and with that, Mother got up to refill the drinks.

"I'm sorry, you all," Nancy explained with a smile. "There is a convention for funeral directors to attend in New Orleans where you can see the latest and greatest for your funeral business. We just always called it the expo. The official name is the Death Care World Expo." The silence was deafening and even Sarah came to the quilt frame to hear more.

"Well, Nancy, I go to a large floral expo or market twice a year, and it has everything I'd ever want for my shop. Isabella goes to quilt market every fall," I tried to explain to the others. "It's that kind of event, right?" Nancy nodded yes.

"I assume it is a pleasant kind of happening?" Jean asked with a smile of approval.

"Of course," answered Nancy. "Funeral directors have a bloody sense of humor, Jean!"

"That I understand," quipped back Jean with a laugh.

"I love that whole idea, Nancy, and would really like to help you with making those quilts," answered Sue. "Sylvia, perhaps we could have a little workday here or over in one of Isabella's classrooms one day. This would be such a worthy effort."

"Absolutely," answered Mother with equal enthusiasm. "After this wedding, I will have some time, Nancy. I think we all want to be helpful in any way we can."

Just then the doorbell rang and I left the group to go up to answer. It was Bethany Carter, the granddaughter of the Carters next door. She was selling Girl Scout cookies, so I quickly ordered one box of each flavor to make the order as quick as possible. I was just about to join the others when the phone rang. I grabbed the one on the kitchen wall. I was surprised when I heard Sam's voice on the other end of the line. It was the call I was hoping not to receive.

"He left us last night, Anne. He just gave up," Sam said in a broken voice. "He was so tired, so tired, and then he was gone." He now broke into tears and his breathing was intense.

"Oh Sam, oh Sam," I answered softly. "How very sorry I am, sweetie. I'll come to be with you all as soon as I can get a reservation and notify the girls at the shop. When did this happen?"

"About an hour ago," he slowly muttered. "We were told it would likely happen within hours, so we were all here with him. Oh God, Anne, my dad is gone." He broke down once more. "Mother is so upset. The girls are with her now. I'm so glad I was here. I think he waited to die until we were all around him. The pastor from his church was here and he said that is very common."

"His quality of life has been the pits and now he is with God in peace, where there is no more sickness," I said, consoling him. "I love you so much and wish I were there to give you a big hug. I'll call you later tonight to tell you my travel plans."

"Anne, it isn't necessary. You have so many things to attend to," he said so softly I could hardly hear him.

"You and your family are now mine," I stated. "I can't imagine being anywhere else. Go be with them now. They need you. Give them my love and sympathy until I get there, you hear?"

"All right, my love. Call me tonight," he said before hanging up.

He was gone. He was far away. He was hurting and I couldn't put my arms around him. He needed me for sure and I needed him too. I knew what it was like to lose a father. Please God, help them all, I said to Him above.

Mother came up to check on who was at the door and what was keeping me. I broke down in tears telling her the news. I cried in her arms as she joined me in the sadness of it all. She asked few questions before telling me she would tell the others. She thought I should start packing a few things, so I could try to catch a flight out yet today.

CHAPTER 8

Nothing but sad and hurtful memories occupied my mind as I was flying into the Chicago airport. Just the thought of what Sam was experiencing right now brought me back to when Mother came home from the hospital to tell me my father had died. Why wasn't I there with him like Sam was with his father?

The last time I was in the Dickson home was last Christmas when we had announced our engagement. Even though his father wasn't in the best of health, it was a joyous occasion and I was accepted with open arms.

Sam was quiet and somewhat dazed when I arrived. He was glad to see me, but I took this time to get reacquainted with his sisters, mother, a few aunts, uncles, and neighbors. I felt as if I had known them for some length of time. Mr. Dickson chose cremation, so there was only going to be a memorial service for just the family on Tuesday. His father had arranged everything to be quick and private. I was very conscious of Sam having to be attentive to his mother so I stayed occupied with anyone who would talk to me. I stayed in a spare guest room and kept imagining what it was like for Sam growing up in this house.

As I walked down the hall to join them for breakfast on the day of the service, the door to Sam's room was open. It was close to a shrine of little Sam Dickson's life growing up. I didn't dare go in, but could tell the room had not been updated or changed for years. Perhaps they kept thinking Sam would move back one day. Did my room at home look like that? I would have to reexamine that when I returned home.

The service was strange for me. There were lovely flowers arranged around a Victorian antique table that contained his urn of ashes. Alongside it was a distinguished photograph of him obviously taken some years ago. A large rose bouquet from my family in Colebridge joined the other impressive arrangements. Is this all there is, I thought to myself, comparing it to my father's funeral. Then I started to remember all the things Nancy had told us of how personalized funerals had become recently, like they had been in the past. This wasn't likely the case here.

I sat on one side of Sam and his mother sat on the other. The pastor from his church said a few words, and then, to my surprise, Sam rose from his chair to address the few rows of those in attendance.

"Thank you all for coming," he began. "As most of you know, my father was a very private man throughout his life and planned this service to say good-bye to a good life that included having a loving family." He took a deep breath. "I can remember him telling me many years ago at my

Uncle George's funeral that when people look at you in the casket someday, they are not going to recall how rich and successful you were, but they are going to recall how you made them feel in life. They will recall your generosity, love, and kindness that you gave the world, and that is the legacy that you will leave behind. He did that very thing, and I just ask that you all continue to keep my mother and family in your prayers, as we will greatly miss him. Please join us for some light refreshments at our home on this emotional day of joy and sadness." He sat down, fighting back tears. I wanted to take him in my arms so badly. What a lovely message for all of us.

The rest of my visit with the Dickson family was nearly a blur. I came home alone on the plane thinking how lucky I was to be a part of this loving family. I missed Sam terribly, but knew he had to be where he was. I went directly to the flower shop where I was needed and where my mind could easily be distracted. Sally was the first to greet me as she finished up with a customer just leaving the shop.

"Oh, Anne, how did it go?" she asked sadly.

"I'm at a loss right now... give me something to do!" I said, shaking my head.

"No problem there, Miss Anne," Jean said, embracing me. "We have a stack of messages just waiting for you." Her eyes watered; she wanted to say more.

"We have orders and all under control, but your mother has called twice," Sally reminded. "She said your cell was turned off and she is very worried about you."

"Yes, I will give her a quick call, but before I go home, I need to check on our home like I promised Sam," I said, working up a smile.

I made piles of paperwork and e-mailed everyone I could. My message to Mother was brief. I told her we would catch up on details later tonight but that I needed to get to 333 Lincoln.

I left quietly from the shop as the others watched my body move about. As soon as I drove up the drive to our haven on the hill, I calmed down and felt a sense of purpose and love. It was dusk with a beautiful sunset that made the August summer day settle into its beauty. I entered the house to check the rooms that were dimly lit from a light in the lower and upper hallway. On Sam's desk I lifted and admired the handsome photo of his mother and father. Sam was hurting at this hour and far away from my comfort. I knew I needed to get home to Mother, so I neatly arranged Sam's mail to place on his desk.

I walked out the door and slowly sat on the wicker chair near the door on the south porch. I jumped in shock when, to my left, a glass of lemonade stood tall on the wicker table near my chair. It had a nice fresh mint leaf sitting on top of the cool ice stacked neatly in the beautiful glass. Did Mother surprise me with a visit? I saw no cars, and the lanterns to our drive provided the only light. Was it from our spirit at 333 Lincoln feeling my sorrow and pain?

I then put my concerns aside and propped up my feet to enjoy the comfort that Grandmother's spirit was providing me in this hour of sorrow. "Thank you," I said aloud, putting my head back to rest. "I love you, too."

CHAPTER 9

The next morning was spent at the kitchen table bringing Mother up to date on the Dickson funeral and then catching up on wedding details. It was hard to believe that the wedding would be here within weeks. Sue and I were going for our final fitting at Miss Michele's after lunch. Sam was expected back tomorrow and I planned on completing a full day of errands today so I could spend time with him. He may have his own plans, but I was keeping the night free. I wasn't sure telling him about the unexpected glass of lemonade on the south porch would be what he wanted or needed to hear right now and decided I would save that experience for another time.

It was good to have a quick lunch with Sue at Charley's on Main Street and then go to Michele's to try on our dresses for the big day. She was also pleased to get away from Mia, having left her with Aunt Julia to babysit. We were about to leave when Sue said, "Anne, I went to the movies the other night with some girls at work and I saw Sally and Paige. Sally was nice to introduce me to Paige. She is very attractive I must say. She is so different from Sally's plainness." I had to snicker because Sally was one not to wear any make-up. "She is very nice, for sure. You've got all these single girls around you, Anne. Are you sure Sam doesn't have some friends for us lonely souls?" I laughed at the suggestion.

"Well, I'm glad to hear that you, unlike Sally, are never going to be too busy for that opportunity."

"No siree," Sue said with a grin. "I would like for Mia to grow up around a male figure."

"Absolutely," I said. "She loves Sam's attention, that's for sure." Sue nodded.

"I'd better get back to work," Sue said, looking at her watch. "Oh, before I forget, is the rehearsal dinner still at Donna's Tea Room?"

"Yes, indeed," I answered. "It will be here before we know it. Will you be bringing Mia?"

"No," she said, "my neighbor is watching her for me. Thanks for understanding that I think she is too young to be a flower girl in the wedding. She gets enough attention as it is and I don't want anything distracting for you that day. She will be at the wedding, however, under the watchful eye of her grandmother and grandfather. They can't wait. I have to tell you again how honored I am to be in this significant wedding. Thanks for lunch, Anne." Off she went, throwing me a kiss good-bye.

When I finally got back to the shop, Nancy was there chatting with Jean and Sally. She had quilt fabric in her hand so she was likely showing off her latest project.

"Hey, Miss Busy Bride," Nancy teased. "I just brought a sample of the funeral quilt block to show you all. We're leaving tomorrow, but we'll be back next week with the moving van. I got so excited about this quilt after being with all of you Sunday. You are all such inspirations for me. It's just what I needed to make this move more exciting. I'm sorry, Anne, I meant to first ask you about the funeral and tell you how sorry I am."

"Thank you," I said sadly. "Sam's taking it hard and I'm dreading his trip back tomorrow despite how much I miss him. I'm sorry we couldn't do something together before you left, but we just have too much on our plate right now. I promise we will do that before I walk down that aisle." We laughed.

"Hey, this is a really neat quilt block," I commented, taking it from her hand. "Is this hard? So the family name gets written here, right?" I pointed to the plain strip in the center of the block.

"Yes, but it's not very hard to do," she said. "By the way, I got a call from Sue and she is really hyped up over making the baby quilts so that made me very pleased. She wants to get together after the wedding. Well, I have to run. There's much to do. I love you, Anne. Sorry I am not here to be more helpful with the wedding. E-mail or call, you hear?"

We hugged and kissed and the girls reminded her that the quilt in the frame and the Jane Austen girls would be waiting for her return.

CHAPTER 10

M
other and Aunt Julia were excited about visiting my Aunt Mary at her assisted living home in Illinois. The discovery of her existence had not sunk in for most of us. If it had not been for the persistence of her daughter, Amanda, we wouldn't have learned who her biological father was. I was excited about adding that whole new segment of the family to my wedding. Grandmother Davis would be pleased.

"I don't know for sure when we'll return," Mother announced when I came down to breakfast. "I hope we'll be back late afternoon and Julia will want to be home when Sarah comes back from visiting Jim."

"No big deal on your timing," I added. "I am hoping to see Sam when he returns, but do not know his exact plans. Being gone from work this last week has put him behind, I'm sure. By the way, has Aunt Julia said anything about when their divorce will be final?"

"She did, as matter of fact," Mother said, filling the dishwasher. "She made note of that fact to me that she'd still be married to him at your wedding, but the following month she thought the divorce would be final. Do you think they'll sit together at the wedding?"

"For Sarah's sake, I kind of hope they do," I remarked sadly. "Why did he have to misbehave at work like that? Do you think they'll ever be able to get back together?"

"I have a feeling hearing those wedding vows of yours will make them both think a thing or two about it all. Speaking of vows, did you give some thought to what you want to say?"

"Pretty much, unless I change some wording at the last minute." I pictured myself at the trellis altar.

"Your musical trio for the wedding called yesterday to confirm everything. Did I tell you?" Mother looked up to me for confirmation. "They call themselves 'Wings,' is that right?"

"Yes, good. They are quite good!"

"Now we'll have a final count on the RSVPs soon," she noted, going to her list on the counter. "Next week, we meet with the planner at the gardens and perhaps we'll have some idea about what the weather may be by then. Regardless, I still think we need the tent for the refreshments. If it's sunny and hot, we'll need shade and the sides can be open, and if it rains, we'll have shelter and be able to close the sides."

"What would I do without you, Mommy dearest?" I kissed her on the cheek. "You have thought of every detail while your daughter runs between the flower shop and 333 Lincoln."

"Better get used to that, my dear." She sat down for a moment. "I just hope you'll come to see your poor old mother on Melrose Street once in a while."

"Well, I'm sure you'll keep a quilt in the frame in the basement to work on and we'll have our haircut and lunch appointments together, not to mention me picking you up for the Jane Austen Club." Her smile back to me was comforting.

My day at the shop was distracting with one problem after the other. It started with Jean calling in sick with the flu. The next call of the day was an unhappy vendor who did not get a payment. It was followed by a couple more unhappy companies who were in desperate need and threatened to hold any future orders until they were paid. I felt the urge to argue, but then checked to see that I had totally ignored a nice little stack of unpaid bills, due to my neglect and distractions of the wedding. I had to remind myself I had a business to run and no one cared if I was getting married or buried. I found myself getting annoyed at walk-in customers wanting this and that, which delayed what was already on my plate. It must have shown because Sally offered to stay out front while I tackled business in the back room. Finally the call came that turned my day around.

"Hey, sweetie," Sam's voice announced on my cell when I answered.

"Oh, Sam, how are you?" I asked as calmly as I could.

"I'll be better when I can hold you in my arms tonight," he responded. "I should get to the house around seven if traffic allows. Can you get away?"

"Wild horses couldn't stop me! Where are you now?"

"I'm still at the airport," he reported, sounding more concerned. "It's raining like crazy here and I hear it's doing the same there in Colebridge. I hope I have no delays."

"Sure, just keep me posted. I'll be at the house plenty early to welcome you. Do you want me to pick up pizza or something to eat?"

"I don't think it'll be necessary, Annie, plus I plan on nibbling on you," he said teasingly.

"Ditto, my love. See you tonight!" Dear God, I love that man!

CHAPTER 11

It was seven forty-five, and no Sam. I told myself I would call him if I did not hear from him by eight. I looked out and rain was pounding down. I hadn't experienced such a storm like this at 333 Lincoln. We did indeed need the rain. The summer was dry and keeping things green was becoming more and more of a challenge. I paced up and down the stairs looking out of various windows in case I could see any sign of him. From the second floor I could see some of the street traffic, which was sparse. Now the thunder and lightning became so intense that it made me wonder about Mother's safety. Did she return from my Aunt Mary's before it all got so bad? I went to the phone on Sam's bedside table to call her.

"Are you okay?" I asked when Mother answered.

"Why, yes, Anne," she said calmly. "Are you okay? Aren't you with Sam? Where are you?" She finally let me answer.

"I'm at the house, but haven't heard a word from Sam." I clearly sounded nervous. "He should have been here at seven."

"Well, there surely were landing delays with this storm, don't you think?" she replied, trying to console me. "I just heard on the TV that there are tornado warnings for this county. You know to go under the stairway if it gets bad, remember? We also shouldn't be talking on the phone with all this lightning, so we'd better hang up."

"Oh, I doubt if it will get that bad, but you have a point," I said, trying to give her some comfort. "I may spend the night here so don't worry about me, okay? Please be careful and alert should there be a tornado siren that goes off."

"Sure. Good-night, Anne."

I hung up the phone and headed to the kitchen to get a glass of wine. I had just picked up a full glass when a huge strike of lightning lit up the kitchen. It startled me so much I dropped the glass and heard it shatter on the stone floor as the lights went totally black. The only light now was coming from additional strikes of lightning. Candles. Did Sam even have candles? If he did, where would they be?

I couldn't even begin to wipe up this mess. I must avoid stepping in the wine so I don't drag red spots of wine and fragments of glass to the rest of the house. Where in the world was he? My cell phone was in my purse on Sam's desk in the study, so now I had to carefully step far enough away from my disaster, take off my shoes, and get to the study. It was at this moment I thought of asking the spirit of Grandmother to help me, but that was a stupid thought.

I carefully felt my way into the study, knocking into a few things, but not causing any more disasters. My phone lit enough for me to call Sam's number—which told me service was turned off. Great. What next, I thought? I backed up to the leather couch behind me and sat down. I grabbed the afghan thrown over the back, curled up in the corner of the couch, and watched nature's show of ice and fire. I held the afghan over my head as if it would protect me. I said a prayer to keep Sam, my loved ones, and even 333 Lincoln all safe from this violent storm. The gradual silencing of the storm breaking made me fall into a light sleep.

"Anne, Anne, where are you?" I heard yelling from the distance. The lights were still out despite the storm breaking so I wasn't sure I heard what I heard. Was I dreaming? "I'm here. Are you upstairs?" Sam's voice repeated, moving about the house.

"Sam, oh Sam! I'm in here!" I responded as loudly as I could. "I'm in the study on the couch. Don't go in the kitchen. I'm in here!"

I saw his figure approach me and I wanted to break into tears of joy, but my emotions were so messed up they didn't know what to do first. He threw the afghan aside and grabbed my body.

"Are you okay, Annie?" he said close to my ear. "I'm sorry I was late, but they wouldn't take off in Chicago until the storm had passed. I didn't know if you got tired of waiting for me and went on home. I couldn't get cell service—everything is messed up. Have you been here all night?"

"Yes, and I'm never leaving," I cried, putting my head on his shoulder. "It was a horrible storm and the lights have been out a long time. Please don't let me go. I dropped a glass of wine onto the kitchen floor after a loud clap of thunder and lightning. I'm so sorry, but there is wine and glass everywhere and I couldn't see to clean it up."

"Never mind about that," he whispered, comforting me. "We'll get that in the morning. Let me take you up to bed. Can you walk?"

"What if I said no?" I teased softly, like a little girl.

"Then I would have to do what most rescue folks do and that is this!"

He picked me up in his arms in one big swish of strength and proceeded to come out of the study and headed up the long stairway. I was caught by surprise and hung on tightly around his neck in disbelief. This was better than any movie hero I had ever observed! I giggled with delight as he laid me down on his bed.

"This is where you should have been in the first place," he commanded.

CHAPTER 12

The sun shining into the bedroom put me into the reality of where I was and how I got there. I turned over to see the empty space where I was certain my Sam had been during the night. I glanced at the clock and hoped I wasn't reading it correctly. It was nine o'clock, which was past my normal time to arrive at the flower shop. This was not good with all I had to do. I pulled myself out of bed and grabbed a blanket to drape around me. I went to the bay window where I could see Sam walking the grounds, picking up tree limbs that were scattered in the driveway. How long had he been up and did he have the luxury of a good sleep? I headed to the shower and quickly dressed in my wrinkled clothes. Oh great, I said to myself. Wine had spilled on my jeans and part of the tee shirt. Wishing my clothes had already been moved to 333 Lincoln, I was forced to wear them until I could get home to change. After I made up the bed I was so graciously invited into, I headed down the stairs. I couldn't resist the smell of coffee coming from the kitchen. When I approached the entrance, I was pleased to see the broken glass and wine were gone. This man was amazing. How long had he been up? I took my coffee out onto the front porch, hoping to get Sam's attention.

"Hey, you've got company, remember?" I yelled loudly enough for him to hear me as he stood near the potting shed.

"Good morning, my lady friend," he greeted, as he walked to the porch. Taking the coffee cup from my hand, he said, "Is this for me?"

"Only after you greet me more warmly and friendlier."

He set down the coffee to hold me in his arms. "I don't want you leaving this place anymore, Annie," he whispered in my ear. "This is home now. I hope you realized that after last night."

"Not so fast, Mr. Dickson," I corrected him. "I am still Miss Brown and I don't go sleeping around just anywhere."

"Well, Miss Brown, by the looks of things, you appear to have been in a drunken brawl last night." We looked down at my wine-stained clothes. We both laughed at my frightful state.

"Is the potting shed okay?" I queried, getting more serious.

"I'm afraid it isn't." He paused. "Well, you'll be the best judge of that, but I know there is one broken window and some things blown over from the storm."

"Oh, no," I said, turning from him to check it out.

"Not so fast," he warned, pulling me to sit next to him on the wicker couch. "We have more important things to talk about—like us, for instance. You stay here and I'm going to join you with a cup of coffee."

51

"Okay," I offered, trying to slow myself down. "You're still the boss here until next week, I suppose."

While he was gone, I called Sally at the shop to tell her where I was and why. I said I would be in after I went home to change from wine-soaked clothes. She laughed with amusement and assured me the street was quiet, but there were many tree limbs scattered down Main Street. She said the shop was fine and the telephone was quiet.

"Jean will be in at eleven so I should be fine. Why don't you take advantage of this week and get some more things moved? There is no reason for you to be here unless we get some emergency orders. The Clever funeral flowers are ready for Kevin to deliver when he comes in shortly. Oh, I almost forgot to tell you. There is a message on the answering machine from Ted."

"Ted, did you say Ted?" I repeated.

"Yup, your once long-ago lover, Ted," she explained with exaggeration.

"Good Lord, what did he say?" I asked in shock.

"It was short," she noted. "He just says, 'Hey Anne, it is Ted. Give me a call if you're not too busy.' That doesn't sound too urgent or anything."

"Well, I am a little busy these days so I'm not sure that will happen."

"Whatever. I'm just the messenger," Sally stated.

Sam then joined me on the porch. He was talking about the weather and how lucky we were that none of the bigger tree branches fell last night. I decided very quickly I wasn't going to tell him about Ted calling the shop. Sam was such a confident and secure man that it would be hard to get his jealousy worked up. He knew very well in the beginning of our relationship that I could have easily gone back to Ted. He now sat down, put his feet up on the railing, kissed me on the cheek, and began drinking his coffee.

"I talked to Sally and things are under control there so I think I will go home to change and then bring back another load of my things. I think this is a good day to start filling my clothes closets since I didn't have anything to put on this morning."

"Good idea, Miss Annie. I like it." Sam put his arm around me. "The moving van comes Saturday, am I right? Do you have an idea where you want everything to go?"

"Yes, actually I do, however, I think a woman has every right to change her mind should I see it looks bizarre!" I gave him a flirtatious smile. "I can't believe this is all really happening, can you?"

"It comes and goes with me. When Jim told me that Thursday would be my bachelor party, reality did have a check, you might say. I guess Thursday's better than the night before the wedding in case we have a little too much toddy."

"Yes, that is a good thing, but what in the world do you think Uncle Jim has in mind for that night?" I questioned, now feeling concerned.

"Nothing for you to worry your little head about. It's guys from work. I did gather that. Maybe there will be a nice little naked lady coming out of a cake like they do in the movies." He loved teasing me.

"If Uncle Jim is in charge, who knows what will happen, so be careful and don't do anything to break a leg or screw up the wedding in any way."

He laughed and gave me a warm kiss on the lips that was enticing, but Sally's voice and my shop responsibilities rang in my head. What happened to the responsible lady of Brown's Botanical?

"Okay, I hear you," Sam now seemed to pick up on my subconscious thoughts. "I wanted to share one more thing before you go. You've been very understanding about not having a honeymoon planned because of my father being so ill, but I want you to know I have a short honeymoon surprise for you. It's not far, but I know you'll love it. We'll have some quality time together before our lives get so caught up in our responsibilities after the wedding. This house, my job, and your shop are enough to swallow us up if we aren't careful!"

"Oh Sam, that's wonderful." I reached for his hand. "Just tell me how many days to prepare for and I'm all yours. Wow, a Dickson honeymoon—that's a surprise to my wedding agenda for sure. I can't wait. Can't you drop me a little hint?"

"Nope, and don't try to seduce it out of me," he said, drawing me closer. "Plan a good week away with casual clothes or no clothes." He never ceased to delight me.

CHAPTER 13

Mother was glad to see me come home and Mr. Carter was already busy picking up tree limbs in the neighborhood. She was also pleased to find I was taking the day off to further my move out of the house. She offered to fill her car and accommodate me on my trips to 333 Lincoln. The weather was beautiful after such a horrendous night.

Each time Mother and I unloaded another trip of clothing and small boxes, she was enthralled with the amount of space that Sam and I would have in our large home.

"So there will be empty rooms with nothing in them for now, right?" Mother asked, putting the last of the clothing into one of my spacious closets. "You'll have to have a big family, Anne."

"I didn't hear that, Mother," my voice echoed from the hallway. "How about I get some lunch and we enjoy it under the gazebo today? The temperature is marvelous. I'll call Sam.

He may want to join us on a lunch hour from the office."

"That sounds wonderful, Anne, because I'm not dressed to go to a restaurant, that's for sure. I'll check out the damage you mentioned in the potting shed and see if I can help clean that up a bit."

"You are a dear, Mother, but I don't want you working this hard," I scolded her as I went to get in the car. "I'll be right back. I'll grab some deli sandwiches at the IGA. Sam has tea and lemonade in the refrigerator, I'm sure." I waved good-bye and headed to the best local business in the city of Colebridge.

The IGA grocery store had been in business for many generations and local families lived off of their fresh homemade deli department each day. I knew my mother went there every other day of the week. I suppose my new role as Mrs. Dickson would have to support the store as well, starting today.

I was waiting for fresh sandwiches to be made, along with their wonderful mustard potato salad, when a voice startled me from behind.

"Make mine a tuna salad sandwich," said the surprisingly familiar voice of Ted Collins. I jumped.

"Oh hi, Ted," I quickly responded. "I didn't see you here. I'm picking up some lunch for Mother and me. How are you?"

"Pretty good, I suppose, under the circumstances," he said sarcastically like I quickly remembered from the past. "Did you get my message?"

I decided to lie. "I haven't been to the shop today, Ted. I'm moving things out of Mother's house and she's helping me," I said, putting my containers in the cart. "You called?" I now left the counter for others to move forward.

"Yeah, I did," he answered, with some anger in his voice. "I really felt I wanted to talk to you one last time before you decide to be Mrs. Sam Dickson." I stopped to give him a puzzled look. "I guess I just wanted you to know that my feelings have not changed despite your wedding plans. Everyone tells me how happy you are, and when I hear that, it still hurts." Now I wanted to run out of the store without paying.

"I don't know what to say, Ted," I said in a low voice, hoping no one was picking up on our conversation. "I am happy and want you to be happy for me. Besides, I thought you and Wendy were practically engaged."

"I think you know better, Anne," he retorted, staring straight into my eyes. "You haven't even known Sam a year and we had quite a history together." Now he was directly in my face. I took a step back.

"Okay Ted, I get it, and I'm glad you are concerned about me, but I wouldn't agree to getting married if I were not certain, so give me some credit here. I think you'll be just as happy one day. Don't lay this on me days before my wedding when I have so much on my plate and so much to look forward to."

"Okay, I get it too, Anne. Or is it 'Annie' now?" He was getting more sarcastic. "I just think you'll be sorry one day. Excuse me for caring and have a nice day!" He turned around sharply and walked into the crowded aisle.

I paid and rushed out to the car, where I sat in total dismay. I had to digest what just happened. I felt such a combination of anger, sadness, and pity. I thought he would have more class than this. Did he actually think I would change my mind and go running back into his arms, right here in the grocery store? Any guilt I had breaking up with him had now turned into disrespect and anger.

On my way home, going down Jefferson Street, I saw a big SOLD sign in front of the large yellow brick house that now was sure to belong to the Barristers. It was a reminder to call her this evening to catch up. She was just the person to tell about this last minute visit from Ted.

When I arrived with the sandwiches, I took them into the house to fix our drinks. I placed everything on the tray. I could still feel how unnerved I was as I carried it to the gazebo. With Mother out of sight, I decided she must be in the potting shed. I quickly found her sweeping away and getting dirtier by the minute. I had to chuckle to myself as I had not seen my mother work in such dirty conditions ever!

"Holy cow, Mother! You don't need to do all that," I chided, stepping inside from her pile of leaves.

"You know, Anne, this feels so good," she commented, wiping her forehead. "This is kind of fun. I can see why you like this little shed tucked in your backyard. You have it fixed so cute as if it were your little dollhouse that you used to have at home, remember? I have more clay pots in our garage at home if you want them. I wish I knew the names of some of these plants. I did help myself to some of your herbs out there. I hope you don't mind. It's good they get cut back once in a while, you know!"

"Mrs. Brown, you are something and what a help this is!" I gave her a little hug. "This shed is a little slice of me for sure and I'm glad you see it, too."

"Planting ivy in this old shoe and geraniums in this wash basin, how clever! Are these the gardening tools you received for your birthday?"

"Yep. Pretty cool, huh?" I was careful in not saying the giver's name. "She was with me one night last week when I came home so sad from the Dickson funeral and I found it very comforting."

"You really did?" Mother shook her head in disbelief. "I don't know what to think anymore!"

"It couldn't be anyone else. Who else would comfort me with a lemonade cocktail on the south porch? It was well received and I told her thank you."

"Oh, for heaven's sake, let's eat this lunch you brought." We laughed and shook our heads going out of the shed toward the house to wash our hands for lunch.

"Everything is on the picnic table," I said as I picked up some napkins. "I have lemonade or tea."

"Some of Grandmother's lemonade will be just fine."

After we ate our sandwiches, we settled in on the wicker chairs on the south porch. I asked Mother about her visit with my new Aunt Mary. She said she was doing poorly and didn't think she would come to the wedding. She thought the commotion and being out in the heat would be too much.

"I wrote to Helen Dickson and told her that I would have their family over for a light supper the evening of the wedding," Mother announced. "Julia said she would help me. I don't want to send them back to the hotel even though they may want to go back for a short rest."

"You said you might do this, Mother, and I think it's a wonderful idea if you don't think it's too much work. They'll love it and Sam will appreciate it as well. It will make me feel good that our family will be all together. Oh, Sam said he has a little honeymoon surprise for me. Now that his father has passed, he feels we can get away for a little while. I am so excited. I hope I don't work those girls to death at the shop. Sue said she would work a day and Aunt Julia would babysit Mia for her."

"Hey, I can help at the counter too, you know," Mother remarked, perking up at the thought. "I was pretty darn good at the bookshop." It was good to see her so happy and she was indeed helpful to me.

"Oh, while you were at the IGA, the UPS man came with another wedding package, so I put it on the dining room table with some others I saw you had received."

"I can't believe all this is happening, can you? I think we'll have a little gathering to open all the gifts when Sam and I return from our honeymoon."

"That would be lovely," Mother gave me a big smile of approval. "Don't forget, tomorrow we go to the park to make sure everything is ready."

"Everything is ready, Mother. Everything." I said, grinning with happiness.

CHAPTER 14

I watched Mother write the final check to the wedding coordinator in the park office. It was all becoming very real now. First came the wedding shower and now my mother was paying for something that had to really happen. Hmmm...

"It all sounds like you've covered everything," I complimented. "I've been watching the weather. It may be a bit cloudy, but the good news is that there is no rain predicted."

"Have you been in touch with the reverend, Anne?"

"Yes, of course. Don't worry. He's done many weddings here at the garden."

"Okay Anne, we must go. The moving van comes in a half hour," she reminded me.

We headed home and I commented to Mother that today had so many big changes that were exciting yet frightening. Just as we pulled in the driveway, the moving van began to position the truck for loading. We jumped out of the car and opened the front door to the house.

"You direct them with your things upstairs, Anne," Mother began, ordering me like she had rehearsed it all in her mind. I did as told, like every day of my life.

Two burly, nice men came up the stairs and I told them what all needed to go. I assured them I would meet them at 333 Lincoln to show them where they were to put the furniture. As they took away my bed in pieces to the truck, I choked with emotion. I went into the bathroom to contain myself. If Mother saw me like this it would make it ever so much harder for the both of us.

After I contained myself, I looked again at my empty room. Only the faded furniture outlines on the carpet remained. This seemed to be my room forever. A flashback was taking me back to all the drama I experienced here, as I threw myself across my bed. It was in this room that Mother told me my father had gone to heaven, like I was a little child. It was here I stayed awake at night trying to convince myself that Brown's Botanical could really happen. It was here I came home with a pearl and diamonds on my finger as I accepted Sam Dickson's proposal of marriage. Now it was here where my next chapter would begin.

Observing Mother with the boxes she had assembled, I could tell she was nervous and doing anything she could to keep busy. She was even offering refreshments to the movers, which they turned down to save time.

"I'll have some of that ice tea, Mother." I entered the kitchen. "Perhaps you should put a little vodka in with that." She looked at me unsure of what I had said. I gave a nervous giggle and then she knew she heard correctly. At that moment, we both acknowledged how hard this morning had been on both of us. I broke into light tears first, which made me angry. Mother followed, but tried to be the brave one between us.

"We knew this time would come, Anne, and it's a happy occasion," she reminded. "I dreaded and yet wished for this moment for you. I am so happy for you. Sam loves you so much and has embraced our family. What more could a mother want?"

"Is there anything in the basement that goes?" one mover asked.

"Oh, I'll go look," I quickly offered as I dabbed away a tear from my cheek. "I don't think so, but let me make sure."

I walked slowly down the stairs that I had run up and down thousands of times in my life. Below was my floral quilt in the frame. It was almost done. I walked around to observe the entertainment furniture that I nearly wore out growing up. When I saw the gas fireplace, I recalled how Grandmother Davis used it to communicate with us when we sat around the quilt frame. I saw the tray of thimbles Aunt Marie brought, just waiting for the next quilter to try on. Oh, Aunt Marie, I thought. We all miss you. You got us all quilting right here in this basement. I can still feel you here!

I saw the counter area where we decided to keep our wine and on-going delicacies that we nibbled each time we were together. I snickered to myself when I recalled how Aunt Julia did not want us to have wine anywhere near her quilt in case we had an accident. That had changed quickly when we started experiencing the spirits in this room. We couldn't keep enough wine on this counter, and if we didn't supply it, Grandmother Davis or Aunt Marie did!

"Anne," Mother called, coming down the stairs. "Did you find anything else to go?"

"No, Mother." I fought back tears going up the stairs. "I want everything to stay exactly like it is." She knew and felt my thoughts.

"Do you want me to go with you over to the house to help when they unload?" she offered with such sincerity.

"No," I said, shaking my head. "I'll have to take it from here." How true those words were going to be from now on. As someone once said, "It's time to put on your big girl panties."

Still trying to be that big girl as I drove from Melrose Street, I answered the ring on my cell phone, hoping it was Sam to cheer me up.

"Hey, Miss Brown," the female voice said strangely, "It's me, Sue. I'm over at Aunt Julia's and we decided to invite you to a little 'girls' night out' tonight." We know Sam will be with his guy friends, and you shouldn't be somewhere thinking about what he may be up to. We've called a few friends, including Nancy, who just got back in Colebridge by the way. We told them to meet up at Charley's at eight. Brad is working so he said he'd save us the round table near the bar. He even teased us with saying he'd be our designated driver. Are you there? Are you listening?"

"Thank you, thank you," I said as gleefully as I could. "I've been feeling crappy and anxious all day! Moving my things out from home has just been the pits. My nerves are in shatters. I'd love nothing more than a few drinks with my friends. How cool it is that Nancy's back. I was going to call her today. I will be there with bells on." I hung up feeling eighteen again. There would be life after 490 Melrose Street! This was just what I needed.

To my delight, when I drove up the hill, I saw Sam's car.

He was already helping the moving van concerning where to park. I got out and went over to kiss him on the cheek.

"I had to be here, Anne, to make sure this was all really going to happen," he teased. "This day is really something! I can't believe you'll now live here with me."

"I know," I said in a more serious tone. "It has really been emotional for me. Sue just called to say the girls are meeting tonight for a few drinks. I really need this."

"Good," he answered, giving me a hug. "Now I don't feel so bad meeting up with the guys."

"Where to, Mr. Dickson?" the movers yelled. Off we went to give directions for our new home and all the other duties for the rest of the day.

CHAPTER 15

Mother teased me as I was getting dressed to meet the girls. I tried to look as attractive as I could, but I was more the tailored Ann Taylor girl and not the glitzy girl that single life seemed to attract. I told Mother she could join us but she was insistent this should be a girls' night out with no restrictions like a mother in the room. I agreed.

Nancy was the first to see me arrive at the bar. We hugged and reminded each other that once a "Mrs." appeared in front of my name then life would not be the same. I greeted Sally, Jean, Aunt Julia, Gayle, Sue, and a few women from Main Street that Sally got to know. I didn't see Paige. As I moved about to check out the room, I saw Kevin.

"Hey, I'm single and likely to stay that way, so I told myself I was entitled to have a beer or two with you guys!" he said happily, like he already had a few beers. "I'm so happy for you, my lady," he said, giving me a hug.

"Thanks, Kevin," I said, hugging back. "I'm glad you're here. My family at Brown's Botanical is pretty special. We've been through a lot."

"Yeah, and I've brought a share of trouble to you too!" he shot back, reminding me of giving work to a guy named Steve, who tried to harm me.

"That's water under the bridge," I confirmed, as I eagerly took my glass of merlot from Brad.

"Before you all get three sheets to the wind, I want to make a toast," Sue announced, raising her glass of white wine. "Here's to the best friend we all have and may she be happy with her future husband, Sam." They all cheered loudly.

"Here's to all of you that I love so much!" I responded, joining them in another swallow.

"I say we toast the flower delivery to be on time for the wedding!" announced Kevin in a slur. We all laughed nervously.

"You guys better not screw things up," I warned with a tease. "Please, no joke playing or I will have a heart attack."

The table was getting more and more crowded with folks who knew some or all of us. I saw Nancy walking toward the restroom and decided to join her. When we were alone inside, I told her about running into Ted and what he said.

"Oh, Lord," Nancy responded. "He just wants to rattle your chain. He knows you have no doubts and he wants to remind you that you were the one who broke up the relationship. He wants you to feel bad. That way, if you have any marital problems, he can say 'I told you so.' What a creep. The rumor has been that he's engaged to Wendy Lorenz, is that true?"

"He says not, but word has it that Wendy is at least telling everyone that they're engaged," I said, laughing at Wendy's

presumption. "They deserve each other, so I hope it's true."
We then started telling stories about when I first met Ted
and she met Richard. She was just what I needed to make
this special night about me and not the future Mrs. Dickson.
Walking back to our table, Nancy said, "So help me,
Anne, if you get pregnant before me, I am going to be quite
upset with you."

"You need to forget about that mission, Nancy, and let
things just happen," I advised. "When you think about
things too hard, they can't happen. I love your plans for
funeral quilts, and I can see us working together on that,
even from the flower shop perspective. If you throw yourself
into all that, a baby will come. You don't have to worry about
Sam and Anne Dickson. If I have my way, the children will
have to come in another life."

"What do you mean by that?" she asked with a horrid
look on her face.

"What I'm saying is we have no plans for children." I
said bluntly.

"Does Sam know that?" she asked with the same look.

"He does love children, that's for sure," I said with a smile.
"It's just not possible for a good while. I need to focus on my
business, and as long as he travels like he does, we have no
business having children. The mere thought of it scares me
to death!" I could tell these words shook Nancy, who really
didn't want to hear what she heard.

"What a jolly good time," Jean said coming toward me.
"Maybe we should spike up the tea at our Austen Club, do you
suppose?" We both laughed in agreement. "I should get on about.
Al is probably having a tizzy by now, but I don't want to leave."

"Then leave you should not, Miss Jean," I said, ordering

her another drink.

"See that gent over there with the scarlet sweater?" Jean asked, pointing with her glass of wine. "When he turns about, check out his back porch. It's plump enough to make your shackles rise! Would you agree, Miss Anne?" We laughed and I nearly choked, swallowing the wrong way.

"I agree," I said. "Miss Jean, you shock me! I think you are enjoying your night out without Mr. Al!" Aunt Julia overheard and joined in our silliness and laughter.

"I may just introduce myself to that gent," suggested Aunt Julia, who was starting to feel her alcohol.

"Aunt Julia! You wouldn't!"

"You dare me?" she challenged, now holding her chin up bravely. "He appears to be the right age, too."

"No he's not," I said quickly. "He's way too young for you, plus your divorce is not final yet."

"So is that a blatant dare, Miss Anne?" asked Jean, trying to encourage Aunt Julia.

"Okay, Mrs. Baker, you're on!" I said daringly, in hopes she would not take me up on it.

Off she went. It was just what she was waiting to hear. We all gasped at the sight, but she did indeed introduce herself, and the group of men around seemed to welcome it. Watching her, I realized Aunt Julia had put off fun and approval from others long enough. As I watched the flirtation and influence of alcohol float about the room, I wondered what Sam was doing. Was he using good judgment or was he too taking dares as a soon-to-be-married man? I did enjoy seeing this social side of so many folks who meant a lot to me, but I was really ready to turn in my single license for a married one. Yup, this all could be so much more fun with Sam by my side!

CHAPTER 16

꙳ ꙳

My cell was ringing on the bedside table in the guest room where I was deep in sleep. Out of one eye in the dark shaded room, I looked to see who was calling.

"Hi honey, it's me," Sam said with alertness. "I'm up and at 'em here getting some packing done, so I thought I'd check in with you. How was last night?"

"You talk too much," I warned, wanting to just turn over and go back to sleep. "What time is it anyway? My room is dark and I'm still asleep. Call you later." I hung up the phone to go back to my dream.

My cell rang again sometime later, and when I picked up, it was Sally checking to see what time I would be in. I did have to get into the shop today, and told her that after some coffee, I would be there. How could three glasses of wine knock me out like this? Come to think of it, two glasses were normally my limit. I showered and took an aspirin for a dull headache that did not want to go away. I knew a cup of coffee would be just the thing.

"Well, sleepyhead, good morning!" Mother greeted me with coffee in hand. "You must've had a good time last night. I didn't hear you come in. Do you realize that this is the last day you will be known as Anne Brown? Tomorrow's the big day!"

I sat down to absorb her words and drink a few swallows of the hot liquid.

"I should have gone for my walk today instead of sleeping late." I agonized over my choices. "Sally called and there is much for me to see to at the shop. I'll have to do my packing for the trip later. It shouldn't take long. Sam said to just bring a few casual clothes."

"So you had a good time with the girls?"

"Oh, sure," I said with a cluttered mind. "We did have a good time and lots of folks showed up. I wonder how Aunt Julia is feeling today. I think she will adjust quickly into single life again. It was fun to see her relax and have a good time."

"Well, she's not single yet, may I remind you," Mother clarified as she refilled my coffee cup. "Can I do any laundry or anything for you this morning? I'm going over to Sue's for dinner tonight. Ken and Joyce will arrive this afternoon. Aunt Julia and I are bringing some dishes to help her out. Would you like to join us?"

"Goodness, no," I confirmed, trying to get out the door. "I want to see Sam sometime today. I hung up on him this morning when he called earlier."

"No, no. You can't see the groom before the wedding! It's bad luck."

"You have that wrong, Mother. It's the day of the wedding

71

you aren't supposed to see the groom." I laughed at her caring humor that I loved so much.

"Okay, so don't say I didn't warn you!" She now turned away to unload the dishwasher. "There are a couple more gifts to take to 333 if you're going by there today. I'll be getting my hair done this afternoon, but if there is anything you think of for me to do, just call."

"Thanks. I'm off. Love you, Mother dearest!"

When I arrived at the shop it was buzzing with activity. I was glad to see everyone had shown up after our party last night. After saying hello to customers that didn't expect to see me there, I went to the computer to check the e-mails.

"Anne, I didn't know if you were coming in, and when you said you were, I still wasn't sure whether to tell you what I found with the mail," Sally slowly commented as she sat down next to me. "Kevin said I should have waited to say something until after the wedding, but I didn't agree."

"For heaven's sake, tell me what?" I asked sharply, not being in the best of moods.

"This note obviously came in the mail slot like the others, only it's on different paper." She handed me another hand-printed note like I had received from a guy named Steve, who I had hired and fired months ago. They were threatening notes and eventually the police found him and served him with a fine and a small amount of jail time. According to Kevin, who recommended him, he felt Steve had moved on from the area. The note only said: *BACK AND BOLDER!* Kevin then came into the shop from the truck and shook his head in disgust.

"You didn't need to see this, Anne," Kevin stated. "I haven't seen him anywhere and he probably got wind of you getting married and he just wants to make you uncomfortable. If I were you, I wouldn't tell Sam. If you want to let Officer Wilson know again, it wouldn't hurt, but the less we make out of this, the better."

"I couldn't agree with you more, Kevin, so you all need to keep this quiet. I may tell him later when we get back from our honeymoon. I will have to call Officer Wilson, but Kevin, if you see this guy anywhere, please phone the police so they know he's around here again."

"For sure, Anne," he said in agreement. "How are you feeling this morning, by the way?"

"I'm good, but not great, let's put it that way," I said quietly. "I must remember the dangers of that third glass of wine." Sally and Kevin laughed.

"Does Jean know about this note?" I asked quietly so she wouldn't hear from the front room.

"No, she came in later, remember?" Sally reminded.

"Good, the fewer that know, the better."

When they each left the room, I took the note and hid it in the rear of one of my side desk drawers where no one would come across it. This was no doubt annoying, but no one was going to ruin a perfectly planned wedding for me. I had to leave a message for Officer Wilson, and at least I had the incident reported. I continued on with my e-mails and came across one from Ted. It read, *You know I wish you all the best. How could I not? Love, Ted.* Well, that was a nice note, or was it? Hmmm...

My next thing on the list was to confer with Sally that all the flowers were here and in order for the next day. She had put my headpiece ring of white lilies, baby's breath, and sprinkles of pearls aside for me to take home. It was precious, to say the least. My hair would be down and my off-the-shoulder white satin dress with the pearls that Sam had given me would be the perfect match for the look I wanted.

"You best be getting on to tackle your chores for the big day," said Jean, also now looking at the flower ring. "You will be the most beautiful bride ever, Miss Anne. I have a lovely new dress for the garden affair. Even Al is a bit excited, by golly!"

"I'm glad. It is all exciting, isn't it?" I mused, smiling with the thought. "I do have to go get my nails touched up and then go by the house in hopes of seeing Sam. I think Sally has everything under control, don't you Sally?" Sally nodded and then gave me a hug.

"Don't you worry about a thing. I mean that," she reassured me.

"I hope you'll bring Paige to the wedding tomorrow."

"Thanks! She would love to be there if she doesn't have a date."

Driving from errand to errand, I couldn't help thinking about the stupid note left for me at the shop. My biggest concern would be Steve doing damage at the shop or 333 Lincoln. If he knew I was getting married, he would know I'd likely be gone for a while.

I pulled up the drive at 333 Lincoln and, to my delight, saw Sam's car. I loaded up my arms with packages and more last minute clothing as I saw him approach me.

"Here, let me help," Sam said, eagerly kissing me on the cheek. "You just caught me between trips."

"I'm so glad to see you, although Mother said it was bad luck that I was seeing you today before the wedding." I kept chatting as we walked into the house. "Hey, what smells so good?" I walked toward the kitchen and Sam followed.

"Blackberry pie from Mrs. Brody." Sam was patting his tummy with a smile of approval. "It's our wedding present. She also left a card. I hated to dig in without you, but man, does that look good! Have you eaten lately?"

"No, as a matter of fact I haven't, and I'm starved. What a sweet thing to do for us, Sam."

We rubbed our hands in anticipation and decided to enjoy the homemade pie that had a perfect-looking pie crust right out of a magazine and plump berries likely from the property behind us. Sam poured himself a glass of milk and I put a cup of instant Starbucks in the microwave. We made our way to the south porch where the breeze was steady. As we caught up on Sam's bachelor party and my girls' night out, we couldn't seem to let go of each other's hands. The love of the pie, our home, and good conversation made me feel we were already Mr. and Mrs. Dickson. This Kodak moment would hopefully be a snapshot of what was to come.

CHAPTER 17

I woke up in our spare bedroom early on September 12, my wedding day. I mentally did a walkthrough of the day's events and repeated, as always, "This is the day the Lord hath made; let us rejoice and be glad in it." I put on my robe and knew when I walked down to join Mother for breakfast it would be the last time, after living in this house my whole life. She was surprised to see me so early, but she still had managed to have coffee ready and waiting.

"We had a nice visit with Ken and Joyce last night," she shared. "Sue is so excited about the wedding and could talk of nothing else. I saw her dress. What a nice touch with the red ribbon with all that white."

"Yes, she will have a little red in her bouquet. She will look beautiful, I'm sure. She said she lost a few pounds chasing after Mia, so I think she'll look great in that dress. The limo is picking her up before us. Mia will go with Uncle

Ken and Aunt Joyce. I bet folks will be surprised to see you are giving me away, don't you think?"

"I don't think they'll be surprised at all, Anne. You have always done your own thing." She put her arm around me. "I am indeed honored. Does my hair still look decent from my appointment yesterday?".

"Of course," I rushed to the refrigerator. "I hope my flower ring survived and doesn't need refreshing." I found it in excellent condition, thank goodness. "After I eat this muffin, I'll shower and be ready for that wedding dress, Mother. I hope it still fits. Maybe I'd better not eat this muffin, come to think of it."

"You must have something on your stomach, Anne, or you'll faint."

"Every time I think of having to repeat those memorized vows, I want to faint. Why did I ever agree to do that? I wonder if Sam will remember?"

When Mother had finished dressing in her ivory linen suit, she joined me in my room to help where she could. We were short on words, not wanting to bring on any tears. She zipped my dress and connected my necklace. I suggested she wear a single strand of pearls to complement her classy suit. She then took the flower ring and placed it on my head with the short veil turned back. As I turned toward the mirror, I couldn't believe I was seeing Anne Brown as a bride.

"Oh, my dear Anne, I wish your father could see you now!" Her eyes watered, but she held her composure.

"Well I know Grandmother Davis and Aunt Marie can see me, so why wouldn't my own father?" I gave her a smile. "I know he's here in spirit, I can feel it. That's why I just couldn't ask any other male figure to give me away." The doorbell rang.

"It looks like the time has come, Anne, and we don't want to keep Sam waiting!"

We slowly looked about the house making sure not to forget anything, and when I walked out the door as Anne Brown, I felt I was entering a dream from which there was no return. I joined Sue in the rear seat of the limousine for the ride to Bloomfield Gardens. The clouds in the sky were there as predicted, but there were pleasant temperatures with a small breeze. The limo driver knew exactly where to drop us off and the coordinator was waiting for us. We all carefully got out of the limo and peered down into the gardens that had turned into a white fairyland. Attendees were chatting as they took their places in the rows of white chairs. Each row had a white bouquet at the end of the aisle. The altar trellis was incredibly beautiful and I saw Sally fussing about with all the flowers. The white runner was ready and waiting for me to approach. The light music was reaching all the way to the top of the garden, where we waited to get our signal. Any passerby would have been delighted. I had to remember that the park could only seclude the sunken part of the garden for our event. The hillsides could easily be viewed by the public, who might want to take a peek as well.

As the coordinator moved us down the path where we would approach the runner, I became so lightheaded that I wanted to beg for a chair. Was everyone here? Where was Sam? Who else could be watching us? Would Ted be brave enough to come? Would the horrible Steve be behind the bushes and be bold like his note said? Oh, the vows. Will I remember them?

"There's your hubby-to-be, Anne," Sue said with excitement.

"He looks great! So does Uncle Jim! I hope Mia will behave. It looks like my dad has all her attention. What if she cries when she sees me walk past? Did you see her in her dress?"

"I can't take it all in," I fluttered to myself. This is where the runaway bride would make her exit, I reminded myself. Then I thought of Sam. "Seeing Sam is the most important thing, Sue. He's really here!" I took a deep breath. "I don't know if I can do this, Mother!"

"Yes you can, Miss Anne," she said as she kissed me on the cheek. "I think we'd better not keep them waiting. They're all starting to turn around and Sam and Jim are looking at us." Mother tried to move me forward. The music was playing for Sue's entrance. Oh no, the wedding had begun. I would have to really do this! I knew I would need help, so I prayed like I had never prayed before.

"Okay, walk slowly and take a deep breath," Mother whispered as we started our walk arm in arm. "You'll do fine. Keep your eyes on Sam. Doesn't he look handsome in that white tuxedo?" She kept whispering things to keep me calm as I smiled and walked toward Sam. I didn't want to make eye contact with anyone else, but out of the corner of my eye, I could see Aunt Julia winking at me. Sam was now next to me, taking my arm from Mother. Mother kissed us both and Sue took my bouquet to start the ceremony.

CHAPTER 18

Pastor Hamel greeted us casually to put us at ease. He began with a simple prayer. I was shaking badly. Could I still be a candidate for a runaway bride? "Calm down, Annie," Sam whispered. "We're going to do this together."

We went through the steps as we were told by the pastor. The vows I wrote were now spoken a bit differently, but who would know? After that hurdle, I could feel my pulse calming down. My role in this play was nearly over. I now could listen intently to Sam's lovely words. The string instruments were sending soft lovely music in the background. The ceremony was happening just like I pictured it in my dream, only it was now becoming a reality. Now and then a sniffle came from Sue and Uncle Jim consoled her. Goodness knows what was all going through my family's minds as they watched us take this final step.

"Anne Louise Brown, do you take Sam William Dickson to be your lawfully wedded husband?" Pastor Hamel's lips and mouth had asked. Was this the time? Did I hear correctly? This was the grand finale that tested every notion in my head. I was leaving Anne Brown behind at this altar.

After stares came my way, I knew it was my time to say something. Finally. I very quietly said, "I do." Sam tilted his head like he didn't hear me.

"Sam William Dickson, do you take Anne Louise Brown to be your lawfully wedded wife?" the pastor continued.

Sam firmly answered, "I do," as he looked directly into my eyes.

"I now pronounce you man and wife," Pastor Hamel said with a smile of completion. "You may now kiss your bride." Sam not only kissed me but grabbed me into an embrace of delight, which surprised me. I wanted to say something, but was so caught up in the exercise and drama of it all. We then turned to face the crowd. Mother was the first to catch my eye, and she was wiping away tears that held a million memories and emotions.

"Ladies and gentlemen, I present to you Mr. and Mrs. Dickson," the pastor announced to the guests. The guests now clapped and cheered.

Sue was the first to hug and kiss each of us before we walked back down the aisle. Uncle Jim was next to congratulate us.

"Don't screw things up like I did, Sam. You've got a great girl here!" Uncle Jim said with a look of regret on his face.

We then approached Mother and Mrs. Dickson, who were both anxious to embrace us. This was all like a scene that I was watching from above. I wasn't quite sure what everyone was saying. What was going through Mother's mind right now? Was she missing my father as much as I was right now? We walked slowly, nodding to folks that were blending together in my watery eyes. The reception area by the tent had guests lined up for us to greet. Aunt Julia was near sobbing when she gave me her hug. Sam's family, the few that were there, were all welcoming me with hugs and kisses as they teased Sam. Jean and her husband, Al, were very complimentary with their wishes. It was my chance now to tell my staff how gorgeous all the flowers were. Nancy and Richard seemed to be so thrilled to be there.

Nancy kept repeating, "You did it, Anne. You did it!" She knew me well enough to know this was not an easy step for me to consider. I introduced Sam to Richard and I could tell we would become compatible as a foursome. When Kevin, looking incredibly handsome, bent down to give me a kiss, I whispered in his ear that I wanted him to check 333 Lincoln every day in case Steve would do something foolish there. He asked if I told Sam and I swayed my head to the contrary. Sam looked puzzled but kept the line moving. The guests were served champagne immediately following the ceremony so the party had begun as they followed through the receiving line. All this planning and I could see the finish line coming way too quickly for this lovely lawn party. Mother and the Dicksons were mingling nicely and little Mia was running around entertaining many for attention.

"I love you, Mrs. Dickson," Sam whispered in my ear when there was a break in well wishes. Why did he have to gloat on the new change of my name that I had forever?

"I love you too, my love," I whispered. Keep smiling, I told myself. This is the day of my dreams, remember? I left that single Brown lady standing at the altar.

Then the many toasts began. I think, by the many comments, Sam and I had surprised many friends and relatives by giving up our single lives. It appeared that everyone loved a wedding, indicated by the laughter and cheers. The chocolate and raspberry cake from Nick across the street was over the top. I knew he would make it extra special for me. I didn't want the traditional look, so the red raspberries on the white icing gave it that delicious look, instead of the dreaded white wedding cake. We did the ceremonial cut and licked our fingers in delight. The photographer didn't miss a pose through the whole ceremony. The photography service was a gift from Aunt Julia who knew the photographer. How well she knew him, I wasn't sure. He was her age and a good-looking man. She seemed to hang near him and offered him a glass of champagne, which he refused. Uncle Ken and Aunt Joyce were having a marvelous time with their granddaughter, Mia. Sue made a beautiful maid of honor for me. She was enjoying the much-needed compliments on herself, as well as the darling daughter she could now show off.

"Anne, can I get you anything?" Mother asked, looking quite attractive as the mother of the bride. "The food is delicious. How about having me bring you a sample? The lemonade is a nice touch, but I thought we decided on cranberry punch."

"I didn't order lemonade!" I answered with a puzzled look.

"Well, it's delicious and quite appealing served in that gorgeous crystal punch bowl," she described. "With the white lilies around it, it is beautifully done. The caterer has outdone himself, don't you think?"

"Did you say white lilies are by the lemonade, Mother?" I asked, walking into the tent to see for myself. I stood there and stared a moment.

"Can I pour you a glass, Mrs. Dickson?" asked the waiter.

"Why yes, thank you," I answered, trying to digest it all.

Others were now crowding around, including Sam.

"There you are, sweetie," Sam put his arm around me for the photographer to snap a photo. "No champagne?"

No, I was too thirsty. "This is quite good," I answered. Sam then turned to greet some folks from his office and I went back to this paranormal happening at my wedding.

I knew Grandmother had her hand in all of this. She just had to make her presence known once again. She knows that lemonade is significant to me. Aunt Julia and Sarah now came near me to compliment my dress.

"We need to do a little toast to our loved ones who are not here, Aunt Julia," I stated, looking rather serious.

"We do?" Aunt Julia teased. "Can I drink my champagne instead of this lemonade?"

"Grandmother has provided us with lemonade and white lilies, so take it all in," I said, nearly in tears and turning away from them.

"Oh, my word, Anne, not here," she said quietly for Sarah not to hear. "I'd better stay away from that. Have you tasted it?"

"It's quite good, as always," I said, trying to get a grip. I lifted my glass in a toast, looking up.

We both laughed and shook our heads, knowing this was neither the time nor the place to discuss our spiritual friends. The chatter and merriment around us was all quite pleasant. I would catch Sam looking at me at most anytime as he engaged with the guests. It was nice meeting some of his folks from Martingale that I hadn't met before. I sat down for a moment to give my toes a break from my new shoes and noticed Sam was moving in my direction.

"I think it's time for the honeymoon couple to get into the limo. What do you think?" He came closer. I was thinking the same thing in my mind and nodded with approval as he kissed me for the hundredth time that day.

Sue then pulled me aside and reminded me to throw my bouquet when we ventured up the hill to the limo. Was this going to be her big moment perhaps for her future? Very few single women were in attendance, so she probably had a good shot at making it happen.

Aunt Julia had gathered less than ten single women to see us off and wish for their wedding to perhaps be the next. Surely Aunt Julia was not considering herself free at this time! She announced it was time for the bouquet to leave me. Laughter and excitement awaited my throw. I faked a movement with my hands, only to catch them off guard. Then, I gave it a slight toss. "Yea!" was among the screams, and then I turned around. With complete delight, it was Sarah holding my flowers! Aunt Julia made some remark about trying again. I went to Sarah and hugged her with my happy approval. She was on cloud nine!

We joined our mothers to tell them of our plans and the looks on their faces were a combination of concern, sadness, and happiness all rolled into one. They each said their good-byes with hugs and kisses for a great trip. I started to walk away and then just had to turn around to Mother one more time. This Kodak moment was gut wrenching.

"This is not goodbye, Mother. I'm not going away," I said, tearfully, as I hugged her one more time.

"I'll see you next week, sweetie. Take care. I love you and will miss you. Please be happy." She turned away with tears as she tried to be brave. Sam watched with concern as he led me to the limo.

CHAPTER 19

The limo took us to 333 Lincoln where we would change our clothes and take off for this unknown mini trip. It was somehow magical going up the hill as Mr. and Mrs. Dickson. Anne Brown was happy here too. Would I miss her? Sam was the first to get to the door and announced that he knew it was tradition to carry the bride in the doorway. I laughed at his attempt, hung on, and we landed on the couch in the study.

"I think I've done everything right to get you here, Mrs. Dickson," he teased with another kiss. "Welcome to our home!"

"Oh Sam, I love you so much," I said as I pulled off my headpiece. "It was a lovely wedding, don't you think? I am quite pleased with myself that I didn't break down on a few occasions. Poor Sue, our mothers, and Aunt Julia were crying every time I glanced at them."

"As much as I would love to spend our first married night here, I think it best we get on our way before dark," he said, removing his coat. They are expecting us this evening with a candlelight dinner."

"Who is expecting us?" I asked, now with more interest.

"No one we really know," he said. "It's a service I have arranged, so I'm anxious for you to see the place."

"Well, let's hit the road," I suggested, heading for upstairs. "My jeans are ready, just like you recommended."

"Do you have something like hiking shoes?" Sam wanted to know. "I think you'll want to take them."

"Well, I don't think Missouri has any mountains nearby but I'll take your word for it," I said with a grin. "This is getting more interesting. We're going to have a candlelight dinner with blue jeans and hiking shoes?" He laughed, chasing me up the stairs.

It was dusk when we left in Sam's SUV and the night had a nice chill to it. We talked nonstop about the reception. He confessed he was worried about how his mother would do after such a short time after his father's death. He thought the merriment was helpful to her and commented about how well she got along with my mother.

"Did you happen to see any conversation between Aunt Julia and Uncle Jim?" I asked out of curiosity.

"I did see a nod to each other when they came through the receiving line, but who knows what they may or may not have said," he observed. "Sarah, I'm sure, had to have contact with both of them. Who knows? They may all three be together right at this moment. Weddings do strange things to people."

"Oh they do, do they?" I asked, wanting to know more.

"Do you think this wedding will have us doing strange things?"

"I wouldn't be surprised," he teased. "You continue to surprise me and we have our whole life together. Change is good. Growing together is good. I can't wait to find out what it is going to be like having you to myself under the same roof!"

During the drive and with all our chatter, I wasn't paying too much attention to where we were going. It appeared to me that we were getting further and further out in the countryside. There was a beautiful full moon that held the light where all appeared to be very dark. The roads were starting to wind in more and more dramatic curves that went up and down. It was beautiful Missouri at its best.

"You do know how to get there, right?" I teased once again. "Will it take hours to get there or are we getting close?" He laughed in amusement.

"Somewhere in between," he teased back. "Just relax. If you get tired, just take a snooze."

"Not on your life," I said boldly. "I am on my honeymoon and I don't want to miss a minute of it."

Some time later, we drove up a steep winding hill. It led us to a structure that was either a large private contemporary home or a lovely country club. The glass and wood structure with sleek lines was lit up with only two cars parked on its lot.

"We're here!" announced Sam with delight. "Welcome to The Quarry House."

"The Quarry House?" I repeated. "What is The Quarry House?"

"Wait until you see this magnificent place, honey," he

said with excitement. "We are located on top of a cliff that overlooks a huge quarry. Wait until you see the view! I heard about this place and checked it out. I have it booked for just the two of us this week."

I was trying to get into the excitement with Sam, but when he said just the two of us in this isolated area, I had mixed emotions. We were greeted by a handsome, dark-skinned young man named Carlos. He took our bags and led us into a unique and amazing house. As Sam and Carlos talked, I was totally blown away with the very modern architecture, spacious ceiling line, sleek furniture, and colorful glassware that seemed to radiate off the pure white walls. The rooms were open and large beyond belief. Our master bedroom was up in a loft that had every comfort and convenience possible. It looked down to walls of expensive artwork that Carlos said was mostly from local artists.

"What do you think, honey? It is all ours for now. Wait until morning when you can see the view."

"It is absolutely divine! I don't know what to say," I responded with delight.

"I take it you work here on a regular basis, Carlos?" I asked, wanting to know more.

"Yes, ma'am, and my wife, Cecelia, will be your maid and serve you your meals," he explained. "She's in the kitchen preparing your dinner and will serve it when you are ready. If you need us at any time, just pick up any of the phones. We live nearby and will be at your service. I'll be happy to pull your car into our garage, Mr. Dickson, if you'll give me the keys."

"Thank you, that would be good of you. We'll freshen up a bit and then be down for dinner."

When Carlos left our bedroom, we looked at each other, not knowing what to say or do first.

"This is a marvelous place, Sam," I said with admiration regarding his find.

"This is where our life begins, Mrs. Dickson," Sam said with such conviction. "It will be an adventure and I can't wait!"

After we got refreshed, we didn't want to keep Cecelia waiting, so we walked downstairs to the dining room, which was surrounded with glass walls. The candles were lit on a glass dining room table held up by a huge rock platform. Cecelia introduced herself and graciously took our wine order. She was also dark skinned, a short, somewhat plump woman, who was very pretty and a good match for her husband, Carlos. The couple was going to be an interesting component to the week at hand. I brought my book to journal and my story had begun.

After a light meal fit for a king and queen, we took our wine glasses out to the patio off the living room. In a far, far distance one could see a few lights, but the moon and stars were the only lights in our little heaven. I had to admit that Sam had bravely chosen a unique environment for our short getaway. This was romance at its finest. The wine, the meal, and a full, packed wedding day made it easy for us to turn in for the evening. Sam's gentle approach to our lovemaking made for a perfect night that I wanted to remember forever.

CHAPTER 20

It was hard to sleep late with the morning sun and an enticing smell of breakfast coming into our room. We decided a good morning walk around the beautiful grounds would be first on our agenda. It was hard to leave this home, or our bed for that matter, where our needs were met with every comfort. I wanted to sneak a phone call to the shop but thought, in all fairness to Sam and myself, I needed to relax, refresh, and concentrate on being a married lady. Sam did check his phone several times, but I pretended not to see. If I contacted the outside, it would be kept from Sam.

We came back for lunch after a short walk around the premises. The hearty, delicious lunch almost required a healthy walk. After checking in with Carlos, we decided to hike the cliff in the afternoon, which would take us to the very top of the quarry. Carlos said the next day's forecast was rain with possible storms, so we wanted to take advantage of the gorgeous day. We dressed accordingly and I couldn't remember when I had put on my hiking shoes last. Sam looked adorable and was the perfect looking Mr. Outdoors. I had to play a role I was unfamiliar with, but that was okay. At least my daily walk had me somewhat toned for the challenge.

The cliff was quite steep and the path going upward seemed to be quite traveled, so we supposed we could handle the task. It didn't take me long to huff and puff, but Sam pulled me along like a good and loving husband. Our hill at 333 Lincoln wasn't quite the same as this. We finally made it to the top, teasing each other about becoming two old people rather quickly. We sat near the edge on the very hard rocks, looking into the deep rocky quarry. One would not expect to see a sight like this in Missouri. It would be typical and unnoticed in the western part of the United States. After drinking from our water bottles, we touched on our short bucket list of things we wanted to yet accomplish in life. Getting settled at 333 Lincoln would have to be addressed for me when I got home. Sam had already settled in there ahead of me. I teased him about disrupting his nest to incorporate a wife. I told him I wanted to start furnishing the living room with some of the money that Mother had given us for our wedding present. We both loved antiques and shared ideas about what would look good where. I was getting pretty excited about it all until he asked what room would make the best nursery.

"Nursery?" I asked with a half smile. "Well, if that should ever be needed, the maid's room off the back bedroom might work."

"It has to be in a room next to ours, don't you think?" he said so seriously.

"If we have to do any construction to make it next to our

room, we should keep that in mind."

"I think we have tons of other projects to address before designing a nursery, don't you?" I suggested lightly, without trying to make it such a heavy topic.

"Look, we both have to be on board here, but I don't want you on the pill for very long," he announced, like he had a plan. "Goodness knows how long it may take to become pregnant."

"Yes, Sam," I said firmly, getting up from the uncomfortable rock. "We do have to both be on board here, but I first have to adjust to being married, how it will affect my work schedule at the shop, plus set up housekeeping for the first time in my entire life, much less worry about who would be taking care of our baby." My body language with folded arms and turning a different direction probably said more than I had intended.

"Okay, Mrs. Dickson, I think I got your message," he said with a low tone of anger. "I guess I'm getting ahead of myself. I have this picture in my head of our future. You will always be an independent woman with your own ideas. I have to remember that. I don't see being a mother interfering with that."

"Yes, indeed, you don't seem to see that, do you Sam? I'm not Superwoman either," I reminded him sternly. "I want to know more about my husband. I want to grow things in the potting shed. I want to furnish our beautiful home, and, if I am so fortunate, I would like to grow my business. I just can't think about that right now." By now I was nearly shouting. "I think we need to head back down before dusk."

Sam was silent with his head down and trying to absorb all the things that rolled off my tongue. I brushed myself off. As I headed toward the path, I knew we had just experienced something close to our first fight as man and wife. Sam followed behind me, remaining silent. Going down this cliff wasn't as easy as I thought it might be and I nearly slipped down on my rear end. I turned around with embarrassment to see if Sam was going to say something, and I found him sitting on a rock as if he were out of breath.

"Sam, what is it?" I asked as I walked up a few steps to him. "What's wrong?"

"Oh, it's nothing. Just give me a minute," he said softly. "I've had these little pains before, and no big deal. I thought if I rested a bit they would go away easier. Don't look at me like that, Anne. I said, it's no big deal."

"Good heavens, Sam, how often do you have these pains?" I asked in fright. "Do you think I should get help? Do you want to lie down? How about taking a deep breath and letting it out slowly to relieve any tension?"

"I'll be fine. Chill!" he insisted. "They are passing. I have some pills the doctor gave me, but they are back at the house."

"I'll go get them. Stay here," I commanded.

"No, you're not!" he fired back. "I can continue. It's not as bad as it may seem. I just wanted to calm myself down."

"Did I upset you Sam?" I asked, wanting to cry. "If I did, I am so sorry. I love you so, so much." He shook his head no, without any words.

"Okay, let's go," he said, getting up to finish the journey.

He seemed more himself when we returned to the house but I insisted he lie down after he took his pill while I showered for dinner. All sorts of worried thoughts were going through my mind as I let the water try to wash them down the drain. Was Sam not telling me something in regard to his health? How frequent were these pains? Was he keeping his doctor abreast of his situation? I was going to make it my business to assess it all when I returned home. What else did I not know about Mr. Dickson? Hmmm...

We went down to dinner in a more somber mood. Cecelia had lovely music playing and a clever themed table setting to match her Asian menu for the evening. We shared our merlot and egg roll delights out on the patio before dinner. We watched from a distance the approaching storm that we'd been hearing about. It was an amazing sight, despite its threat of danger. I asked Cecelia about emergency measures and she assured us that they were well prepared with everything including a generator. There were multiple candles burning throughout the house, so if the power went out, we would be fine. The dinner courses were intriguing and very delicious. Sam showed quite the appetite as I watched him closely. I dropped any mention of his health. I had to trust he had it under control. I did not want to be the nagging wife and the independent you know what, all in the same day. This was our honeymoon, for goodness sake. Lord, help us both, I said to the God Almighty upstairs.

As the wind picked up, the sprinkles began. We sat on the sofa with a magnificent view of the storm approaching. The handy binoculars sitting nearby made the scene all the more awesome. When the lightning started, I wanted to get away from the glass walls. Cecelia was there cleaning up the dinner, so I contained my fear of what might yet come. Sam's arm around me was more than loving and reassuring. As the storm grew worse, I suggested we go to our room and climb under the covers. Sam laughed and teased that he was never going to turn down an invitation to get under the covers with any woman. The extra snuggling, as the lightning and thunder roared, was much more tolerated as one!

CHAPTER 21

We slept extra late the next morning after a very scary night of storms, unlike I had ever experienced before. We both felt we were up high enough in the heavens to make it seem as if we were in the middle of it all. The morning had a light drizzle and no sunshine to speak of. I told Sam I would spend my morning journaling in one of the corners of this incredible place. After breakfast, Sam went up to shower and I took the opportunity to call Nancy. I had to talk to someone about what had just happened the day before. When she answered, she spent the first three sentences fussing at me for calling on my honeymoon. When I described the previous day's scare with Sam, she understood completely.

"Sam is not stupid, Anne, give him some credit," she warned. "He saw a doctor on this and has some pills, so let him be the guide here. I agree that you need to be in on this situation, and you can do that when you return home."

"But Nancy, I think I brought on this stress," I confessed. "We were on the top of the cliff having our first disagreement, you might say."

"Was it about who was trying to push who, or what?" she teased.

"I will tell you more about it later, but it was his immediate plans for us to have children," I explained. Just thinking about it made me all frustrated again.

"Oh boy," she said, as if she knew how it played out. "Did you not have this subject come up before now?"

"Not really," I replied, feeling somewhat naive. "He would joke now and then, but Nancy, it's like *he alone* has a plan. I'm talking a real timetable plan of some sort. I need time, lots of time."

"Of course, you do," she said with understanding. "He'll see that for himself in time, Anne. Relax my friend—you're on your honeymoon! Hey, I'm nearly ready to quilt the quilt for the funeral home," she announced, changing the subject. "I can't wait to show you all. I will bring it to the Austen Club next week. Will you be there?"

"Oh sure," I answered as it made me smile. "I promised Mother that the club would be something we would do together, so I will pick her up and be there!"

"Sue and I are meeting at Isabella's tomorrow to pick our fabric for the baby quilts," she said with excitement. "I am so happy she is interested in this because my time is limited and she can work on these at home. By the way, our house is coming along nicely. You must come by as soon as you get home."

"I will," I said, as I wondered how I would manage the time. "I need to furnish some rooms at the house, so perhaps we could be helpful to each other."

"I can tell you right now that I have too much furniture to fit in this house so maybe you could use a thing or two," she offered.

"That really sounds good, Nancy," I said. "I'd better go before Sam comes looking for me. Thanks for listening. I'm so glad you're here for me, friend!"

"Me too, girl!" she said, laughing. "See you next week."

Sam soon joined me in the den. The comfy chairs and splendid view were so tempting. I curled up and my pen didn't stop as I filled up pages and pages. Sam was reading the paper and then in no time had fallen into a snooze. Yep, this was a Kodak moment into what married life must be like—each of us doing our own thing and yet together. Hmmm...

The relaxing days slipped by. Our conversations perked up, our intimacy got better and better, and there didn't seem to be further indication of Sam's chest pains. When we said our good-byes to Carlos and Cecelia, I knew that I wanted to come back here on each anniversary date. Sam thought it was a great idea. It was very romantic and a step into a place where our daily activities could not interrupt us. As we drove back, I felt relaxed and more aware of the new role I was about to play.

When we arrived at 333 Lincoln, it really was home. We watched each other with the excitement of our new start. I unpacked in unfamiliar drawers like I was visiting someone for a long stay. Thank goodness we each had our own space in our newly remodeled bathroom. When all was put away, I walked to the kitchen to look for a snack of some kind. I opened the refrigerator to beer, white wine, cheese, expired orange juice, and a stale loaf of bread. I went to the pantry to find a nice assortment of spices, cans, and unknown boxes of sorts. Then

I spotted a few apples in a basket on the counter. I grabbed one and joined Sam in the study where he was opening his mail.

"I checked out the kitchen and I'm not sure what I should or should not be doing in regard to dinner tonight," I said, bewildered. Sam looked up and grinned.

"You're off the hook, sweetie," he said, giving me a little hug. "Why don't we check in with our work and meet up at Charley's around six o'clock? I'll have to grocery shop, and you're welcome to join me. I'll cook up something for us tomorrow. Who knows? I might teach you a few things!" I grinned and kissed him on the cheek.

"You'll be getting rid of me within a week if I don't get with the program, right?" I said with some degree of certainty. "Give me a little time, okay?"

"You have the rest of your life, remember?" he said, so sweetly.

"It may take me that long," I kidded. "Okay, I'm going to the shop and will meet you at Charley's. I may go by Mom's and pick up my mail and see how she's doing."

"Great idea," he said, now getting back to his mail.

On the way to the shop, I wondered whether I should have mentioned going by my old house. He was probably thinking how he was going to have to wean me from my old habits and Mother's apron strings.

When I arrived at the shop, Jean and Sally were busily working and were surprised to see me. I received big hugs and lots of questions on why I did not wait until tomorrow to show up as planned.

"I missed you all, if you can believe that!" I confessed. "Did you miss me at all or did you all just goof off? How was business? Aren't you pleased I didn't call?"

"I think we would have hung up on you if you had," said Sally. "You'd better start filling us in on where you went and how it went. We are dying to know every detail."

Gayle from next door came in the door after seeing my car. They all had so many questions and comments about the wonderful wedding. They shared photos and details of the wedding that I had missed in my frightful state. They said my mother had come in to see if she could be helpful and brought them some banana bread. They assured her everything was under control after they shared a cup of coffee with her. When Jean left the room, I asked Sally if there were any more notes from Steve. She said all was well and not to worry about it. I went to check my computer and a well-organized desk awaited me. From all appearances, they were sending me a message that all was well without me.

CHAPTER 22

Instead of running home to Mama, I called her to say we had a wonderful trip and to see if my mail could wait to be picked up. She said there was little mail to speak of, but she did need to meet with me regarding some unfinished wedding details; so I told her I'd see her tomorrow when I picked her up for the Austen Club.

"Are you really going to be able to come?" she asked in disbelief.

"Why wouldn't I?" I asked. "We have this date reserved for us, remember? So we'll talk about any of your concerns when I pick you up, okay?"

"Oh, that's great, dear." She sounded pleased. "I went by your house last week and drove up the driveway, and it looks like you had some damage to the gazebo. I didn't get out of the car, but I'm sure there's an explanation."

"Really?" I was totally unaware. "We didn't notice, but I'm

sure Sam will check it out. Was anyone around?"

"No, not at all. Was there supposed to be?"

"Just Kevin, who was going to check on things," I responded, with worry. "We'll see you tomorrow night. Love you!"

Damage to the gazebo, she'd said. Why did we not see that when we got home? I didn't think the storm was that bad here in Colebridge. Did Steve play some dirty trick on us? Oh, please keep him out of my potting shed. Sam would no doubt tell me about any damage when we met up shortly.

Sam was waiting for me at the bar at Charley's. His warm embrace reminded me how much I missed him in this short amount of time. He had ordered a merlot for me and it was well received, like our ole times!

"I have a table for us when you're ready," he noted. "Well, was it good to be back at that Botanical place?" he teased.

"It was and all was well," I reported as I took my first sip of merlot. "I called Mother before I left the shop and she told me that when she drove by our house, she noticed some damage to the gazebo. Did you see it?" He looked down.

"Yes, I did," he said, taking a deep breath. "Some spokes were knocked out and the table turned over but nothing that can't be fixed. I checked the potting shed and I think it's the way it should be, but you'd have to check that. It was vandalism, for sure, by someone who knew we would be gone. There was something else, too." He hesitated.

"What?" I asked with hesitation.

"The word BEWARE! was spray painted on the floor of the gazebo," he said, not meeting my eyes.

I jolted in anger. "It's Steve; I know it's Steve. He sent me a note like that the day before our wedding. I didn't want to tell anyone. Kevin and Sally are the only ones that knew. It just said, *BACK AND BOLDER!* Forgive me for not telling you. Before you yell at me, I did tell Officer Wilson."

Sam looked like he was going to strike me down, he looked so angry. "Thanks for the vote of confidence, Mrs. Dickson. Did you think I couldn't handle it?" he said with anger. Brad, the bartender looked up at us.

"I told Kevin to check on our place, but guess he didn't know about this," I tried to explain. "Did you call the police?"

"I wanted to break the news to you first to see if you knew who this was!" he said more quietly. "Who knows what this guy is going to do next, Anne?"

"He's evidently out of jail and angry," I shared, taking bigger swallows of wine. "Okay, let's leave this to Officer Wilson. I refuse to live in fear and I'm sorry, Sam, if I made the wrong decision not to tell you. What would you have done? Called off the wedding? Or maybe you would have police guard our wedding?"

"Okay, good point, but the police could have stopped there on their rounds in the evening while we were gone," he said, calming down. "I'll call them tomorrow. I didn't touch a thing. Let's get something to eat."

Needless to say, our conversation was tense because we both were thinking of Steve. I picked at my food and then brought up another unpopular subject. I figured that I might as well be the wife I was supposed to be.

"Sam, are you going to see the doctor or call him to let him know about your chest pains?" I asked, not thinking what the outcome might me.

"If I have something new to tell you in that regard, I will tell you," he answered sharply. "I don't plan on keeping secrets from my wife like some people I know."

Ouch. It now was hurting more than I thought.

"Sam, I worry about you, just like you're worried about my safety with this Steve thing," I explained rather firmly. "You are my husband, but even if you weren't, I would be concerned, so get used to it." He backed up and broke out in a big grin.

"I love you, too, baby," he said, taking my hand to kiss.

"Dessert?"

"The chocolate mud pie, of course." I kissed his hand, too. Welcome to married life, I told myself. Was it always going to be hot and cold? Hmmm...

CHAPTER 23

The next morning, Sam and I assessed the damage done by whomever. Most things could easily be repaired except the paint on the gazebo floor. Sam said he'd have it taken care of. I visited the potting shed and nothing had been touched. It was like checking on my children—a little water here and there but everything was fine.

We sat on the porch to have our coffee and discussed our day's plans. We still had not opened most of our gifts and planned to set a time the coming weekend. I told him about tomorrow's plans for the Austen Club. He said he'd have to go out of town for just two nights but would be home by the weekend. I was relieved because many things needed my attention. He was concerned for my safety and asked if I wanted to stay at my mother's house while he was gone.

"You've got to be kidding me." I was hoping he was joking. "I'm a married woman in my own wonderful house. No one is going to scare me out of my house."

"We need to do the alarm system sooner rather than later, so I'll call them today and maybe they can come soon." I now really liked the idea. "Whatever you decide is fine." I gave him a hug. "I'll be at the shop until I pick up Mother."

The day was going to be beautiful. The lawn service had arrived and I found myself not wanting to go to the shop. I wanted to play house like I had dreamed about. Sam kissed me good-bye and said I should call him when I got home. It sounded weird. It would be my first "home alone" at 333 Lincoln.

The girls were glad to have me back at the shop because the orders were coming in faster than Kevin could deliver. I didn't get a chance to tell Kevin about the damage to the gazebo. He was working double time.

Walking in the house on Melrose Street was a strange feeling. Everything looked the same and Mother was waiting for me with open arms. She had many questions to ask, so I ended up telling her about Sam's chest pains.

"He gets really upset if I mother him on this, so I have to believe he is taking care of this with his doctor," I said with sadness. "We actually had our first fight on the top of the quarry cliff. We are both really independent and this marriage is going to be a challenge, Mother. I hope I am up to the mission."

"You will be, Anne," she said with assurance. "I know how much you love each other. Anything's possible. After a while, you both will settle into your routine and way of doing things. Here's your mail, but we'd better go or we'll miss the discussion on *Pride and Prejudice*." We went arm in arm out the door as fast as we could.

"Jolly good of you all to come," said Jean, trying to get our attention with her little silver dinner bell. "Make sure you get a spot of tea and crumpets before you get comfy. We'll start directly here after we welcome two new chaps: Nancy Barrister and Paige Beerman. Welcome ladies! Sally is going to start our discussion on everyone's favorite Jane Austen book."

Everyone had read the book except Paige, but she didn't seem to mind the early book review.

"I will begin by telling you all that I couldn't help but think of Anne and Sam when I read about the challenging love affair between Mr. Darcy and Elizabeth," she shared. They all cheered. "Two very independent people who found that love could eventually be achieved. Anne and Sam ended up at the 333 Lincoln mansion, but hard to compare it to the Pemberley estate, right Anne?" They roared with approval. I laughed as well.

"I just loved the mother in this book," Mother chimed in, to my surprise. "She wanted those girls married. I could relate to that." They all broke into chatter related to the mother's busybody character.

"But oh, the father, Mr. Bennet," said Nancy with a sigh. "What a trooper he was with all the women in the family. Elizabeth was his favorite, of course, and I could see why. She was so secure in her own right, without a man. She was not silly and frivolous like her siblings. He saw her strength."

Yes, he did, I thought to myself. Did my father see some of that in me? He once told me that no one would be good enough for his little girl, which was similar to Mr. Bennet's feelings. Would he have approved of Sam? My gut told me he would have been disappointed I didn't stay with Ted, who was secure and from a good family. I could almost hear his harsh words at my becoming engaged so soon to Sam. He would have liked him in time for sure, but I would never know.

We continued sharing and it was so fun to be thinking of folks other than ourselves. Our book for next month was going to be *Sense and Sensibility*.

Nancy invited us all to see her house next week. She wanted us to see her funeral quilt and Sue thought if they saw the small baby quilts, someone else may offer to help.

"Don't forget Sunday afternoon quilting for those who can come," announced Mother. "Sally and Paige, we have great snacks and wine, so even though you don't quilt, you may want to come." They shook their heads as they declined.

Mother and I talked and laughed all the way to my former home. I could tell she hated to see me go on my way. How long would it be before she would complain about being so lonely in the big house all alone?

I drove home in a good frame of mind from such a pleasant evening. Turning up our drive to 333, the dawn-to-dusk lights were well received on the dark hill. The thought of Steve came and went. I decided to park the car in front of the house instead of in the garage. Somehow, this made me feel safer entering my new home. I left the south porch light on when I left the house, which led my way into the entry hall. I looked around in disbelief that I actually lived in this great house. I went to the kitchen to grab a glass of wine to take upstairs. The thought of a small wine bar on the second floor was something we might think about for the future. I turned out the light in the kitchen and went up the stairs to enjoy a nice soak in the tub, which I had not experienced before. When I climbed in, I punched in Sam on my cell phone.

"Hey, Mr. Dickson, Mrs. Dickson is reporting in from 333 Lincoln," I said, trying not to laugh. "I am totally immersed and soaking in the Dickson tub with a glass of merlot in my hand." There was silence.

"How can you do this to me?" he teased. "Don't you know I am over a thousand miles away in a stuffy hotel room with no merlot or you in sight?"

I laughed and teased him as I told him about the pleasant evening at Jean's house. I told him we were being compared to Mr. Darcy and Elizabeth Bennet in the book we just read. I explained that they married and lived in a big house. I wasn't sure he was following the comparisons.

As I started saying my good-night, I told him not to scare me with his warnings to be safe. He agreed and proceeded with loving messages for me to take to sleep.

"Are you happy, Mrs. Dickson?" Mr. Dickson asked.

"Yes, indeed I am, Mr. Darcy," I teased.

CHAPTER 24

The wine had put me into a deep sleep. A wonderful dream of cutting beautiful flowers in my potting shed was disrupted by the lights coming on in my room. I quickly sat up as every light in the room was going off and on like an urgent signal. My first thoughts were of an electrical problem. I grabbed my robe, and when I left my bedroom, I was startled to see that every light in the house was behaving in the same manner. I thought of Grandmother. Why was she doing this? Maybe it wasn't her after all. I went to the bay window and I thought I heard a car on the road, but wasn't sure. I walked downstairs to look out from the screened-in porch. The lights stopped blinking. I was relieved and yet very confused. I had to turn on the entry hall light to find my way back up the stairs to my safe warm bed where I could put the covers over my head. I did just that and a deep sleep took me into the morning light. When I awoke at six, which was my habit, I almost forgot about the lights until I put on my walking clothes.

I put the coffee on and pondered what my routine would be for my morning walk. The leaves were already starting to turn. What would the coming seasons be like at 333 Lincoln, I wondered, as I headed out the door and down our hill? I looked for anything out of the ordinary, but to no avail. I walked briskly along Lincoln Street, which was now heavy with rush hour traffic. I should have gone down to Main Street where it was safer and more scenic. I huffed and puffed on my way back up the steep hill, which I knew would be great to keep me in shape.

When I got back to the house, I checked my list of the Saturday errands of the day. I was a big list maker that many teased me about. I glanced around and noticed the furniture was getting very dusty. How was that going to be taken care of? Where was Mother when I needed her, I joked to myself.

Nancy was going to take me to a great antique shop today and possibly a flea market this afternoon, so that would indeed be a treat. Should I feel guilty about the adventure and instead stay home to clean my house? Where would I even start cleaning this place?

Throwing out that impossible thought, I knew my first priority would be going to the shop to make sure all was in order. When I arrived, my loyal crew was all huddled at the front counter in conversation.

"We were just going to call you," announced Sally. "I think we had an attempted break-in last night, but they weren't successful."

"The van is fine, but the back door looks like someone tried to pry it open," described Kevin. "They were likely interrupted by something or realized we had an alarm."

"I remember turning it on when I left," said Sally with fear in her eyes. "We have those signs posted a few places on the building. Maybe they saw one of those."

"Does everything still open and close properly?" I asked, staying calm. "I guess I'll have to call Officer Wilson so he can take a picture and maybe get a fingerprint."

This distraction was aggravating, but I had to take care of it myself since the others were getting busy. When Officer Wilson arrived, he said there wasn't much of anything to get prints on and the break-in attempt could be anyone. Several other shop owners had complained of such incidents off and on throughout the summer. I didn't mention the strange lighting at 333. I wanted to keep these incidents close, so rumors would not circulate about our haunted house on the hill. He didn't give me much satisfaction on the report. Sam would not be happy to hear this.

Closing at noon on Saturdays was a good thing, and Nancy picked me up right on time. There was so much to tell her. The flea market was disappointing with only one flower pot purchase for the shop. It was a darling 1950s white ceramic bunny that would hold a cute little plant just perfect for a nursery. Nancy said she had been saving some unusual pots for me. It was hard to use them for folks when I personally liked them.

The antique shop was some good distance out of Colebridge, but it gave us a chance to talk about when we could get the four of us together. We thought the following week or two would work. As we entered the attractive shop, I saw it was just as wonderful as Nancy had described. I purchased two wing back chairs, two lamps, a couch table, and two marble statues that would go perfectly on each side of the living room fireplace. I decided it all would be from my money in case Sam would think it too much at one time. I didn't like the idea of having to check with someone on how to spend my money. I had a meager salary from the shop, but certainly adequate for a splurge now and then. Nancy purchased small accessory pieces and an odd-looking crazy patch quilt that was narrow in size and had four-inch lace on three sides. As I furniture shopped, she spent a good deal of time in conversation with the shop owner about the quilt. When I approached the checkout counter, I overheard them talking about a funeral parlor quilt.

"What did you say?" I asked the elderly stout shop owner.

Nancy interrupted. "She was told this was used in a funeral home in a nearby town, Anne," she said gleaming, as if this were a rare treasure. "She bought it at the estate sale when the last family member died. Remember I told you these existed at the turn of the century? And the description fits. Picture this over a coffin with three sides of lace shown to the front for viewing. I can't believe you have this. I want this."

"I'm afraid it has a hefty price, ma'am," the owner said with hesitation. "I had to pay a pretty penny myself when I bought it some time back."

"Do you remember the name of the funeral home?" Nancy asked impatiently.

"It was so long ago, I'm sorry, I don't. I wish I had asked more questions, but I didn't. I just knew it was unusual."

"I'll pay whatever you want," Nancy said without hesitation.

I was seeing a side of Nancy I hadn't seen before. She sure

was into quilts related to funerals and such. I guessed it was being around the business after she married Richard. When the owner said a thousand dollars, I nearly fainted. Nancy didn't hesitate one minute and wrote her a check.

I arranged for my delivery to be made on Monday and I was excited beyond belief. When Nancy and I came out of the shop, we looked at each other and giggled with delight at our finds.

"Remember when we used to do a happy dance when we were in high school?" she said, jumping up and down. "I know you think I am crazy, but I got a good buy! You don't just find these quilts every day!"

"Yes, yes," I said joining her as we jumped up and down for joy.

The day was quite fun and I couldn't wait to get back to my new home and plan where I was going to place everything. Sam would be home Monday night and it would be nice to surprise him. After changing clothes, I wanted to go to the potting shed to water some plants while there was still some daylight. Just thinking of the joy it brought me, I got out my journal and went out to the potting shed. I cleared a place to write on the worn, wooden counter and pulled up my stool. The day was cooling down so I left the door and window open to get a clear breeze. I realized I was in heaven. I was always able to write more effectively when I was in a creative environment. It didn't get better than this. I wrote feverishly until I had to turn on the lights.

Realizing time had flown by, I thought it safer to get outside the shed and call Sam like I had intended to earlier. I closed up my slice of heaven and walked into the entry hall. I turned on lights, locked the door, and headed to the kitchen. No food appeared in my pantry, so I decided to have a pizza delivered. At some point, I would have to make that trip to the IGA grocery store like everyone else in Colebridge. I ordered my pepperoni and onion pizza, poured a glass of merlot, and called my wonderful husband.

CHAPTER 25

The night went without incident, and when I awoke fully rested, I reminded myself that it was the last day of being without Sam. The afternoon was scheduled for quilting in the Brown's basement and it was the day the Botanical Beauty quilt would be finished. Would Aunt Julia have a chance to do the binding or would our grandmother's spirit intervene and finish it herself, as she had the others? I was pleased Mother didn't call to see if I planned to go to church. I'm sure she gave it a thought or two. I sat with my coffee and decided I would make that trip to IGA to buy some fruit, cheese, and rolls for us and something yummy from their bakery to take to quilting.

Mother was pleased that I was the first to arrive and very delighted about the cheesecake I brought. We didn't need it with her chocolate pie, but I knew it was Mother's favorite treat from IGA. As we waited for the others, I told her about the wonderful purchases I had acquired with Nancy.

"What will Sam say when he gets home?" Mother asked with such a concerned look on her face.

"He'll love it," I said with a big grin. "He knew I was going to furnish the living room, and besides, I used my money." Mother turned her head like she was questioning my decision.

It was a cloudy fall day and when all arrived to the kitchen, we decided it was a perfect day for quilting. Nancy brought her funeral quilt for everyone to see and they were intrigued to say the least.

"What is it about these crazy quilts?" asked Sue in jest. "Do they all hold such stories and mystery?"

"You had to have a great purse to make one of these," Jean boasted. "They are quite grand and fancy, sort of like the Pearlies in London."

"The Pearlies?" What's that?" asked Sarah, bursting into laughter.

"It's a special day where everyone in the lower class parades around town with outfits embellished heavily with pearl buttons. It's an old, nineteenth-century English tradition. I've only seen pictures. I have never been there in person. It's for the 'toffee-nosed' for sure!" We all became hysterical with laughter.

As we tried to stay focused on getting the quilt quilted, I was asked more questions about our new house. I tried to humor them the best as I could about my wedded life, as Mother was paying very close attention to my every word.

"I was having my coffee yesterday and I noticed dust is starting to accumulate about the house," I teased, waiting for a reaction. I saw Mother roll her eyes.

"I have the perfect char for you, Miss Anne," Jean happily offered. There was silence as we waited for an explanation to follow.

"A *char*?" I asked, trying to be serious. "What's that?"

"A cleaner. You know...I'm sorry," she blushed. "Miss Connie comes to my flat every two weeks to spruce it up a bit. She is quite tidy!"

"Great, could I get her phone number?" I asked with anticipation.

I knew Mother wanted to comment, but held herself back. I'm sure she was thinking about how she sure had raised a spoiled little girl!

"Sylvia, do you think I could use your frame to tie my funeral quilt when we're done with this?" Nancy asked gently. "It works so much better than placing it on a table or floor."

"Well sure," Mother quickly responded. "The frame has been in our family for years. It's open for anyone to use it. Why don't you just bring the quilt top here next time rather than dismantling your house?"

"That's a great idea, Mother," I said with approval. "We are used to meeting here, and we'd love to help you. Aunt Julia, are you still committed to finishing this for me or should I leave it for you know who? If so, don't go home without it." We all laughed but Nancy, who assumed it was an inside joke.

"I took a gander at where it shall be housed in the shop, Miss Anne," Jean revealed politely. "This beauty will certainly strike everyone's fancy!"

"That's the way Anne wanted it," complained Mother. "She missed out on a wedding quilt for her new home with this choice."

"The flower shop is my home...or at least one of them," I boldly stated.

"By the way, I brought some champagne," announced Aunt Julia, out of the blue. We sat silently and waited for an explanation. "The dirty deed is done! I am now officially divorced!" The silence lengthened. I looked to see if Sarah was within ear's reach, but she was upstairs on the phone.

"Aunt Julia, that didn't take long," said Sue on a somber note. "Are you really happy about it?"

"I'm getting happier, let's put it that way," Aunt Julia described. "I'm not proud of it, but I am proud of my self-worth."

"Uncork it for us, Mother," I instructed with confidence. "This is a tough time for you, Aunt Julia, and we want to wish you well. It is a new chapter in your life, and I'm all for starting new chapters."

Mother didn't comment, but opened the bottle and poured the bubbly liquid into our waiting glasses. She reluctantly shared our toast. She always liked Uncle Jim, as did we all, so this was a tough situation for her. This was nothing to celebrate in front of Sarah, however. Nancy looked lost in our conversation, but told her I would fill her in later.

We finished the quilt and Aunt Julia held it up for that celebratory photo. We took turns holding it up. It was beautiful! I made a toast to my dear mother, who appliquéd all the tiny little flowers hour after hour. This Kodak moment had more memories than just a floral quilt for my wall in the shop. It had absorbed many joys and sorrows through its quiltmaking process. Was this still a wedding quilt? Was I really married to Brown's Botanical Flower Shop? Hmmm...

CHAPTER 26

Fall was making its presence known more each day. Sally and Jean transformed the flower shop into a harvest festival. Business was booming, no thanks to me. Sally recommended I find a part-time person sooner rather than later. I hated to add to the payroll, but the additional income could likely handle the extra expense. I didn't want anyone to become burned out. Sue's part-time help to me at the shop was nearly impossible since she had Mia. Sally said she would keep an eye out for possible applicants.

Sam was home for a good many days now and happily encouraged my purchases for our home. He would purchase an item or two on his own now and then, which was always perfectly tasteful. As time marched on, our wedded days were adjusting quite nicely. We both were busy people and considered it a bonus if we could meet up each evening for dinner. Richard and Nancy finally got us to commit to coming to dinner at their wonderful home on Jefferson Street.

"The meal was fantastic, Nancy," Sam said with conviction as he rubbed his tummy. "You obviously enjoy cooking, as do I, by the way. Anne is great at cleaning up while I get to mess everything up."

"She is the best, for sure," Richard echoed. "Now, that's not to say we wouldn't like to sample some of your culinary dishes, Sam. I have also been intrigued with that house of yours on the hill. When we were kids, we'd sneak up the hill to see if we could experience the ghost we would hear about. I guess you took care of that rumor."

"I don't know if we have or not but, if we have one, I think he or she approves of our renovation and love for the place," explained Sam. "Come by anytime and I'll give you a tour. We could do a cookout before the weather gets too cool. Anne surprised me with a great gazebo for my birthday. It's a grand place to enjoy some good food and company."

"That's a super idea, Sam," I added with delight. I really wanted the four of us to become close and entertain together.

"I hear you're quite the handyman, Sam," Richard said, getting up out of the dining room chair. "The previous owner left some interesting tools in the rear shed that I don't know a thing about. Would you mind taking a look at them?"

"Absolutely," Sam said eagerly as he went to join Richard.

"Will you ladies excuse us?" Richard asked politely.

"I, too, want to show you a few pieces of furniture I have put aside in one of the bedrooms, Anne, in hopes you could use some of it," Nancy generously offered. "As you noticed, I have every room furnished here...including a nursery that unfortunately stays empty."

"Everything is perfectly done in this house, Nancy, just as it was growing up with you." She laughed with embarrassment. "Our quilting friends would also be jealous of your incredible sewing room. I'm glad we can get the funeral quilt tied for you on Sunday. I don't think any of us has done that before. We have learned so much in that basement of ours."

"I gathered that." She grinned with approval. "I want to hear more about all the magic that seems to go on there!" I snickered and let the subject drop.

When we opened the spare bedroom door to see her extra furniture, I couldn't believe my eyes! "Where on earth did you accumulate all this, Nancy?" I asked as my mouth opened.

"Believe it or not, our house in Boston was much bigger and I really didn't have time to get rid of anything. Some of these pieces were in Richard's family. My parents always had the latest and greatest new furniture. See anything you like?"

"I like it all," I teased, as I walked over to one of the chests of drawers. "This is unusual, Nancy. One can always use a storage chest. I still have a few empty rooms to furnish. This blanket chest is cool. Why don't I take this? It'll be perfect to store Aunt Marie's quilts that I inherited."

"Take them both," she quickly offered. "I'll have them delivered to you!" I was thrilled to say the least.

After the men joined us in the elegantly decorated living room, we all shared a glass of brandy together before going home. As I looked about, I couldn't help but see the similarities of what you would see in a funeral home. It was way too formal for our taste, I concluded. I was glad, in some ways, that Richard and Nancy didn't have children. It would be more difficult to hold off Sam's notion of a family if we were around them and their children. I was certainly not going to furnish a nursery like Nancy was so bold to do. Our husbands did enjoy the evening together and I would soon plan the cookout at 333 Lincoln.

Sam complained of indigestion going home. We discussed the menu and decided it was the spicy meat sauce on the shrimp. Fortunately, Sam volunteered to tell me he was having a regular checkup at the doctor this week. I teased him about whether married life was more stressful on him than the bachelorhood of his past. He answered with an open-ended answer that said I drove him wild with stress from the moment I met him and had continued to do so.

CHAPTER 27

Nancy spread out the funeral quilt top on the floor of the basement. Everyone admired the precise piecing of what she called an Album quilt. She said in one book, it was also called Chimney Sweep, but she didn't know why. There was a plain strip in the center of each block where a friend or family member could permanently sign their name. The eight-inch pieced blocks were set on point and sashed in plain fabric as well, which would provide room for more names to be written. It was Nancy's intention to list the last names of families who were viewed at the Barrister Funeral Home. The color prints she chose were dark contrast prints against the cream-colored plain fabric. She brought ⅛-inch black ribbon for us to tie the layers together. We helped her position the layers and then Nancy basted an X through the center and around the edges before we pinned it to the quilt frame. We watched in awe of this educated quilter.

Aunt Julia, Mother, Sue, and Sarah were all there to assist in the mission, but Nancy had a handle on it all.

Mia was toddling about, wanting to walk right over our project, until Sue held her. In no time, we all knew enough to secure it in the frame. Nancy insisted on bringing a lovely assortment of treats she personally had baked for us to enjoy as a thank you for the arts of our labor.

"So, Nancy, how will this quilt be used when someone is laid out for viewing?" asked Sue with some hesitation.

"Not everyone will choose to use this quilt, first of all," explained Nancy. "It will be an option for covering the casket or simply displaying the quilt if the person was a quilter or just liked quilts. Most caskets are covered with a spray of flowers. At our home in Boston, we used a quilt with the flowers on the casket and it was quite charming. One person displayed the quilt with an urn of their ashes. It had their photograph on the quilt."

Everyone was now trying to picture the scenarios as they listened in silence.

"I think it will be a wonderful conversation piece in our lobby when it is not being used," Nancy continued. "I want the community to know each family is special and will have their family member's name on the quilt with the date of their birth and death. The baby quilts will be a huge success. I designed a special satin envelope to put the quilt in after the funeral, instead of a covered box. Some may choose to have it buried with the baby. Sue is doing a great job with those."

"They really are darling, and I get teary eyed when I think about how this very quilt will be on some little child's casket or wrapped around them," Sue said sadly. "I'm partial to the little pink ones, because I have a little girl, I guess."

"I'm going over this week to help her," stated Mother. "They are not hard to do and I really feel you are fulfilling a need there, Nancy. You're really to be commended for this project."

"I say we take a break to digest all this," I suggested. "Who wants coffee or wine?"

No one stopped for some time, despite my offer. They seemed to be mesmerized as they were tying each ribbon. It was if they were watching the quilt come alive before their very eyes.

"Have any of you read the book called *The Coffin Quilt?*" asked Nancy as they were still all working. Their stares into space answered her question. "It's a true story, honestly. A lady by the name of Elizabeth Roseberry Mitchell from Kentucky made a quilt in 1839 that documented the family history as they died. She cut out coffin-shaped pieces that were appliquéd in the border until their death. The center of the quilt was designed like a fenced-in graveyard where the coffins would then be placed when they died. Their name would be embroidered on the coffin as well as vines and flowers about the quilt to make it appear softer. There is patchwork and many commemorative symbols on the quilt as well. I'm told it is at the Historical Society in Lewis County, Kentucky. I would love to see it someday."

"Good heavens!" said Sarah in horrid fashion.

"You have to remember that years ago, death was celebrated as part of life!" explained Nancy. "I think we should still recognize it as such."

"I do get it," agreed Aunt Julia. "Marie loved quilts and made so many that we are all enjoying."

"I have the one she made that was what she called a wholecloth," I shared. "She had my name on it because I loved it so much. I always knew I would have an all-white bedroom one day. I cuddle with this quilt often and think of her. Sometimes I think it even smells like her. I think we should make sure our new Aunt Mary's family gets to enjoy one of Aunt Marie's quilts. I know Amanda would love that!"

"That's a great idea, honey," agreed Mother.

The conversation continued with everyone sharing which quilt was her favorite. Even Sarah said she has to have her bunny quilt when she is not feeling well. I continued to be amazed at what feelings were shared around our quilting frame. Aunt Julia's enthusiasm even suggested that the "basement quilters" all make a friendship quilt of some kind in the future. Mother then interrupted us by passing around the homemade goodies, which smelled divine. She continued to caution us to come away from the quilt so we wouldn't have any accidents.

My cell phone rang just as I was about to take my first bite of a delightful chocolate éclair. I had to take the call upstairs to be able to hear the voice on the other end. When I heard it was Officer Wilson, my heart sank.

"Sorry to bother you, Anne, but thought I'd better give you a ring," Officer Wilson said. "It's been noted that Steve has not been reporting to his parole officer and his sister is not talking about where he may be. I called Kevin to see if he knew anything, and he said he just knew through the grapevine that he had been trying to buy drugs, so who knows what that means. My point in telling you this is that you need to be very cautious in case he is still around. I doubt if he's working, so I don't know how he's getting money for drugs. Just be careful, you hear? Let us know if there are any signs of him coming around." I fell silent to a wonder of scenarios going through my head.

"I will. Thanks," I said, hanging up. What it all meant, I had to think about.

CHAPTER 28

When I arrived home from quilting, I looked around for Sam so I could relay the news from Officer Wilson. He was inside the garage rearranging some things and was glad to see me as always. I reported a pleasant quilting session and then told him about Steve. His concern was grave and he cautioned me to be with someone at the shop or when I left the shop. He then brought up the attempt to pry open the shop door as a reminder.

"I know you are used to coming and going as you please, but until this is resolved, you must be careful."

"I hear what you're saying, Sam, but I'll find it hard to do that with my schedule. This creep is not going to invade my life like that. He probably left the area anyway. I promise I will be more careful, just for you." I kissed him on the cheek and started to go back to the house.

"There's some chili cooking on the stove for us," he yelled.

"That sounds great with this cooler weather coming in," I answered back.

I walked into a kitchen full of aroma. I knew how to make a quick batch of cornbread from a box mix, so I began preparing that for the meal that Sam was kind enough to start. Nancy insisted I take some of the baked goodies with me, which I knew Sam would devour in a minute.

After we ate, we grabbed our jackets and sat on the south porch with some coffee. The wind was picking up and leaves were tumbling off the trees much faster than I cared to think about. Sam said he'd have the nursery send over some guys to do leaf pick up in a week or two when the trees would be further along.

"We'd better get that cookout scheduled with the Barristers before Thanksgiving," Sam suggested. "We may also want to think about having a big Thanksgiving dinner at our house. We have lots of room. That table opens up to seat twelve, I bet. Would you be up for that?"

"Oh my." He took me by surprise. "Mother always loved having everyone for that holiday. We also have to think about your mother."

"My point, Anne," said Sam, now standing up. "We have widowed mothers and I figure it's our turn to entertain. I don't know if my sisters will make the trip, but I bet my mother will."

"You're probably right," I said, now giving it some thought. "I think I want to talk it over with Mother though. She has got to be feeling a little lonely right now and I don't want her to think I'm just taking over her life."

Sam looked bewildered. "If you're afraid of the kitchen duty, I'll be happy to be in charge. I've cooked a turkey or two in my day," he bragged, showing his command with hands on his hips.

"I just bet you have, big guy," I teased him. "There isn't much you haven't done. I think we need an early night to turn in. After all, you have a checkup tomorrow so you should be rested."

"I'll turn in early with you anytime, Annie," he said, following me in the house.

We did just that and snuggled under the covers with the gas fireplace providing enough heat to take the chill out of the room. The wind continued to roar as if a storm might be coming our way. It was the best feeling ever to have Sam near me. I now had a difficult time thinking about what it was like with just me lying in bed alone. We had our favorite snuggle positions and special sayings we liked to whisper in each other's ears.

I had just traveled into a deep sleep, when suddenly, we were awakened by lights flashing off and on as if it were a drill of some kind. Sam flew out of bed yelling words that weren't making sense to me. As I sat up to get my senses, Sam put on some pants and went to look out the window.

"Sam, honey, stop," I quickly yelled. "This happened to me when you were gone and it's nothing."

"What is that supposed to mean?" he yelled in disgust. "I'll go out and look around. I don't think this is an electrical problem, my dear. Why didn't you tell me about this?"

I didn't answer because he really didn't want my answer. Before I knew it, he was downstairs and I heard the front door open. What I didn't tell him was that I thought I heard a car go down the hill the last time. I grabbed my robe and joined him on the south porch. The lights had now stopped flashing. Sam had a flashlight, which came in handy as the house now became pitch black. Sam walked toward the garage, obviously worried about the cars. I followed with some hesitation.

"Stay on the porch, Annie," he firmly ordered. I did as he said and waited for his return. I was feeling somewhat confident that things would be okay. I knew it was just Grandmother.

"Check the potting shed," I yelled out to him.

After what seemed a very long time, Sam reported he didn't notice anything wrong.

"I know you won't want to hear this, but I think it's our friendly spirit warning us about something," I spoke between cold shivers. "Remember, she has done this before, Sam. How else can you explain something like this?"

"Well, if your theory is true, what is it that your spirit or ghost is warning you about?" he answered, with anger in his voice.

"Don't yell at me," I yelled back. "Let's go in. I'm freezing!"

We both went into the house and Sam headed to the kitchen. I followed to heat up something hot for us to drink. He went from room to room as if he were looking for a monster behind our furniture.

"When did you say the security guys were coming?" he asked more calmly.

"Tomorrow, to be exact," I answered." "I think it's around noontime."

"We can't be putting up with this kind of nonsense." He fumed, as he drank a swallow of my warmed-up coffee.

"This house has a history and reputation of such nonsense Sam, remember? The flashing lights may be the best security system this house has to offer." His look my way was not convincing, nor did he think it was very funny.

"I'm sorry I yelled at you, baby, but with this Steve guy out and about, we cannot be too careful."

I took his hand and led him back up the stairs to our bed. I fell right to sleep, but I knew Sam was subconsciously guarding the night, snuggled next to me.

CHAPTER 29

S am was still asleep when I woke up wide-awake at an early hour. I quietly changed into my walking clothes and went downstairs to put on the coffee.

I wanted to check some things outdoors in the daylight, like my potting shed. It was a clear brisk morning as I walked around to the side yard. Wet grass and leaves were sticking to my shoes. When I walked into the shed, I was surprised at how many leaves had blown in onto the floor. It must have happened last night when Sam opened the door to the shed. I took the time to sweep them up and watered some plants. It soon would be time for me to bring certain plants inside, like my elephant ears and cabbage heads. I glanced at the place I had recently written in my journal. If I had nothing else to do today, I'd get my coffee and spend another hour or so in my potting place. I did take a moment to plan out my day, which would include talking to Mother about Thanksgiving plans. I did feel somewhat bad about not communicating more often with Mrs. Dickson, so reaching out to her for the coming holiday would be a good thing.

After my walk and kissing my Sam good-bye, I stopped by to visit Mother. Getting an early start to my day was working out nicely. She was where I knew she would be: sitting in the kitchen reading her paper. She was delighted with the unexpected arrival of my visit. She went straight to the coffee pot and offered some of her peanut butter coffee cake.

"What brings you here, Anne? What a nice surprise," she said taking my coat.

"Well, I need your advice on something," I asked as I sat down at the table. "Sam and I were talking over Thanksgiving and he suggested that we entertain the family this year since we have the big house and two widowed mothers who don't need to be burdened with work. Sam said he's cooked many a turkey and would love to do it." I waited for a response. She smiled at me.

"You don't have to check with me about such an idea," she answered. "You know your Aunt Marie and I would take turns to do Thanksgiving and loved doing it, but I think Sam has a great idea there. It will be good for you both to have that first holiday together in your new home. It celebrates you as a couple and it would be fun to share it with you."

"Are you sure your feelings aren't hurt?" I was feeling concerned. "I don't want you to think that we won't be coming here for things. I still want you to have Christmas Eve, Mother, so I hope you'll invite us. I can't imagine Christmas anywhere else."

"Well, I would love to do that, but you must remember Sam has a mother too! The two of you together need to decide these things."

"Oh, thanks. I was worried." I now helped myself to the coffee cake.

My cell was ringing and it was Sue. She was going to go to the Barrister Funeral Home around three in the afternoon to bring Nancy some of the baby quilts she had completed, and she wanted me to go with her.

"Oh, Sue," I responded. "I've been taking way too much time away from the shop and I don't know what our work load will be by then. How about you calling after lunch? Why do you need me to go anyway?"

"Anne, I just feel strange going there, that's all," she said shyly. "Please, please go! Besides, you told her you would. Nancy said she has the funeral quilt done too, so we'll be able to see it. I have to take Mia and you would be a big help there, so please, please?"

"Okay, I'll see what I can do, but I can't promise anything," I warned as I disconnected the line.

"I've got to run, Mother. Thanks for the coffee," I said, getting my coat back on. "Sue wants me to go with her to the funeral home to deliver some of the baby quilts. I wonder why she's uncomfortable to go alone?"

"Who knows, but you should try to do the favor for her," Mother advised. "I can keep Mia if it's helpful."

"No, she'll be fine. I'm sure we won't be there long. Oh, before I forget, Mother, I am looking for a part-time person for the shop if you know anyone."

"Good. I think you could use some more help. Say, what about me?"

"Not on your life, Mother," I tried to picture the thought. "You could occasionally do that, but I need someone with some designing experience. On the retail side, we can train them. I'm in no hurry, but keep your eyes open, will you?" She nodded.

I grabbed some coffee cake for the shop girls, kissed her cheek, and flew out the door feeling better than when I arrived.

When I walked in the door of the shop, a salesman, two customers, and the unhappiest merchant on the street, Nick Notto, were expecting my arrival. I went to my desk, wishing I had come in the back door. Nick immediately sat by my desk and started complaining about a competitor of his that he felt was getting by with murder. He said he had merchandise out on the sidewalk, which was against our guidelines in the area, and he also heard that the same merchant was going to have outdoor music on his patio. Both of these practices were an ongoing controversy in the area. He asked if I would please call the city and complain so the complaint would have more credibility.

"They get tired of hearing from me," he said with aggravation. "By the way, Anne, I've been seeing some guy coming and going around the back of your shop when you're not there. He may be doing some work for you, but I'm here a lot at night and the timing just made me suspicious." I stopped everything and looked into his eyes.

"What does he look like?" I was starting to feel faint.

As he went into his long drawn-out description, I knew it was Steve and now there was no doubt that he was still around. I shrugged off his report, not wanting to draw attention to my problem. I got him to leave when I told him

I had an appointment with my salesman. When he left, I went into the restroom and nearly collapsed. I felt creepy, violated, and angry. Why was Steve not leaving me alone? What had I not discovered? Was I blind to his activity because I really wanted it to all go away?

I calmed myself down and told Kevin to come with me outdoors to look at something. When I told him what had been going on, he became very angry. We came back in the shop and found there was nothing out of the ordinary to report. I went to the back of the shop to call Officer Wilson. I told him to visit with Nick in case anything would be helpful.

I couldn't concentrate the rest of the day and the girls knew something was very wrong. When Sue called to see if she could pick me up to go to the Barrister Funeral Home, I agreed, as I was of no use to my happy little flower shop.

CHAPTER 30

On the way to the Barrister Funeral Home, I left a
message on Sam's phone to tell him I would be
home for dinner. I watched little Mia in her car seat
waving her hands with her gibberish baby talk. Sue seemed to
understand every word she was saying. I wondered, if I ever
became a mother, would I have to drag him or her back and
forth to the shop each day? That wasn't a pleasant thought.

Nancy was looking for us in the grand hall of this historic
funeral home. Folks were coming and going, which indicated
the deceased were likely being viewed during our visit. Kevin
had made a good-size delivery to the home earlier, but I did
not recall the family names.

After Nancy grabbed Mia into her welcoming arms, we
followed her to a small office on the lower level. She said
they allocated it to her since she was going to be involved in
various projects. As soon as we sat down, Richard peeked
in to say hello. He was such a handsome man and always in

such good humor as most funeral directors seemed to be. Nancy adored him and lit up as soon as he appeared.

"Thanks so much for helping Nan with these quilts," he said with sincere gratitude. "She made a significant contribution when we were in Boston so I know the impact of her efforts. Well, I must get upstairs. I'm looking forward to that cookout, Anne. I think you have a pretty good guy there!"

"I couldn't agree more." I smiled in agreement. "We'll do it soon."

Nancy said we needed to go down the hall to one of the workrooms so we could lay out the quilt. I was hoping we wouldn't see anything or anyone being worked on. Sue kept looking at me with slight fear on her face. Mia tagged along, holding her mother's hand as we slowly walked into the sterile-looking room. Nancy went to get her funeral quilt out of a drawer where she had it wrapped in tissue. She opened it up and we helped her spread it out in full view. It was very beautiful and she had finished it with her talented handiwork.

"This is lovely," admired Sue. "I see you already have two names written in this corner. When did you do this?"

"Yesterday," she said with a smile on her face. "Two families are going to be using it in the next couple of days. This afternoon, I will be draping it in a cremation viewing. I had some pictures to show them from our funeral home in Boston, and they liked the idea. They also wanted to have their name written on the quilt. The deceased was a schoolteacher here in Colebridge for some time and a friend of Richard's father. It really adds a personal touch that her name is carried in a memory quilt."

"You really have a heart for this, Nancy," I said, wanting to give her a little hug.

Sue then took her finished baby quilts from her bag and laid them out on the counter one by one. There were two blue ones and two pink ones. How babies could be that small to accommodate these quilts was hard to comprehend.

"Oh, Sue, these are precious," Nancy responded with satisfaction. "I finished the envelopes. Let me get them."

She pulled out another drawer that contained a stack of the blue and pink satin containers for the baby quilts. Across the top flaps were embroidered scripted words that read, "Our Baby."

"I had Isabella's quilt shop do the embroidery," Nancy said. "Didn't they do a great job? If my measurements were right, the folded quilt should fit nicely in these."

She folded the baby quilt in half and then slid the quilt perfectly inside. She closed it with the pretty ribbon bow that was attached on the flap. She looked at it with such emotion. Then I noticed she was tearing up and ready to break down before us.

"I'm sorry. This has such personal meaning to me," she said, now weeping. "We've had a couple of miscarriages and I keep thinking about those little beings of ours who didn't get a burial. They didn't get to be held by the parents who loved them." She sat down with her hands over her face. Now Sue became emotional with tears. I had to absorb what she had just said.

"Oh Nancy, we had no idea." Tears were now coming down my cheeks. "This does have to be hard for you. I see now why you have such a passion and love for those lives that leave us, no matter what age. This is a wonderful thing you are doing in honor of your children you had to leave behind. I really think you and Richard will have your own children someday." I walked over to her and put my arm around her.

"Okay, I'm fine," she said regrouping. "I meant to tell you at some point, Anne, but I wasn't sure when. As I told you, Richard really doesn't want to adopt, so I'm hoping we can still get pregnant."

"Nancy, I have to tell you that precious little Mia would not be in my life without adoption," Sue chimed into the conversation. "I love her as much as my own. If I can ever talk with Richard at some point to be helpful to the subject, I'll be happy to do so."

"Thanks Sue, I'll keep that in mind," Nancy said, wiping her eyes. "We aren't there yet, but you will have no problem convincing me. Thanks so much for making these quilts. Can I pay you somehow for this?"

"No you cannot give me anything for this, but I may ask you to watch Mia for me sometime," Sue said, perking up. "She really has taken to you, and I can tell you love children." I saw a connection going on, and I was the third wheel.

"I would love that and so would Richard," she answered with joy written on her face.

"Well, we need to get going," Sue said, picking up Mia in her arms. "Give Miss Nancy a kiss, Mia. We will come see her again." She not only got a nice messy kiss, but also a hug.

When we got Mia in her car seat, Sue and I looked at each other as if we both needed to take a deep breath from the emotion we had just experienced. It was a good and sobering day. I was glad to be a part of something so personal for people in need. Now thinking back to Nancy, I wondered how I would handle a miscarriage.

CHAPTER 31

S am took the day off so he could meet with the security
company. After I put my car in the garage, I walked into
my perfectly comfortable home and noticed Sam had a fire
already blazing on this chilly night. An inviting smell was
coming from the kitchen where Sam was chopping colorful
vegetables. It was a sight I was used to seeing growing up on
Melrose Street.

"Hey there, sweet Annie. Glad you're home," he happily
greeted. "How does some nice stir-fry sound for dinner? I
thawed out that shrimp you picked up and I think this will
be delicious. So tell me, how was that exciting visit to the
Barrister Funeral Home?"

"I'll be happy to tell you all about it after I pour myself
a glass of merlot," I stated as I pulled out the stopper to the
bottle. "This day was a bag of mixed emotions, Sam. Before
you start the fry, could we just visit by the fire a minute or

two? I just want to warm up in your arms and digest what is all going through my head, if you don't mind."

With that, he looked at me rather inquisitively and washed his hands. He then came my way, brushed my hair to one side as he often did, and gave me a kiss.

"I can see the day was not the best. Am I right?" he asked softly.

I tilted my head to one side, like I couldn't really describe how the day had been. I was hoping to find the words for what I was feeling right now.

"Let me pour myself a glass and join you in the study."

He joined me on the leather sofa, kicked off his shoes, and leaned me back to get eye contact. It was what I wanted but I couldn't relax my body or my mind to begin telling him my thoughts.

"Let me begin by saying that Thanksgiving as you planned will be a go," I shared. "Mother thinks it's a great idea and she agreed that the widows might enjoy a break from cooking this year."

"Great, we'll call my mother later," Sam answered, as if it were no surprise to him. "Then you went to the shop, right?"

I answered with some hesitation and then began my story regarding what Nick had observed at the shop when I wasn't around. Sam squirmed as I continued, but I did not let him interject a word until I was finished telling him and that I had reported everything to Officer Wilson.

"Well, our security system couldn't be timelier," Sam said, sitting up straight. "Please don't go to the shop at night without someone else Anne, until this thing is resolved with Steve," he warned.

"I won't," I said, not wanting to disagree. "I'm so angry

Sam. This is really a pain in the 'you know what' and I am tired of second guessing this creep."

"I don't blame you, honey. So, did you get to the funeral home or not?" I was surprised he was willing to change the subject.

"Yes, Sue picked me up. She had Mia with her so it was good there were all of us. We met with Nancy in her little office and Richard came by to say hello. We ended up in one of the workrooms downstairs, which was very interesting. She finished the large funeral quilt and it did turn out nicely. She already had two family names on it. The really sad part of our visit, Sam, was when Sue showed Nancy the baby quilts she had finished for her. When Nancy was explaining how they were going to be used, she broke down and told us about having had two miscarriages. She just broke into tears, Sam. It was so sad. I had no idea. I don't know why she never e-mailed me about it or anything."

"That is sad," he remarked, not really knowing what he should say. "I don't know how long they've been trying to have a child, but surely they have thought of adoption if something doesn't happen."

"Nancy said Richard was opposed to that, which makes it extra sad and more pressure for Nancy just knowing that her pregnancy is her only chance at becoming a mother. I wish he wouldn't do that. Sue offered to be helpful with any adoption information."

Sam pulled me into his arms and gave me a gentle hug in support of my sadness. There really weren't words that he could say that would be helpful. I knew we were both digesting how any of that information could apply to us.

After several silent moments, we quietly made our

way back to the kitchen where Sam picked up where he had stopped. As he began preparing dinner, I pulled the silverware and plates together.

After we ate our quiet dinner, Sam explained how the security system would work. He made me promise that I would faithfully use its service when I was here alone on nights he traveled. He turned it on for the evening as we headed to our room that was peaceful and calming to our daily stresses at hand. As I removed my make-up, I knew I would have to journal about my feelings sometime soon on these matters. Today's happenings were many pages of food for thought. I told myself I would sneak into the sitting room off our bedroom to write if I couldn't sleep. That did not get a chance to happen. Sam's controlling sense of comfort had put me right to sleep. Any concerns could wait for another day and another time.

CHAPTER 32

The closer Thanksgiving came, the more hectic things became. I still had not hired another person, so with the busy holiday season, I had to make sure my presence was at the flower shop. When I approached the shop at an early hour, I pulled up in front of the shop to find two police cars parked across the street. I said a quick prayer hoping the trouble was not for me. I slowly got out of the car with a handful of paperwork, hoping no one would notice, but seconds later, Nick quickly approached me. He reported that the Spice Shop across the street had been broken into and a sizable amount of cash had been taken out of the cash register. The police were still inside doing fingerprints.

"Is Officer Wilson anywhere around?" I asked.

"No, someone else is, but I already gave them the scoop on what I had observed at your shop," he offered, with excitement still in his voice. "I'm sure it's the same guy, don't you think?" I kept walking in hopes of avoiding further conversation.

"I've got to get busy with some early ordering, Nick, but if you see Officer Wilson show up, would you tell him to stop by?" I walked in the front door, knowing Nick would make it a point to man the street all day if he could talk about this latest occurrence. When Jean and Sally arrived, I had to explain everything.

Sally had anxiously moved a display cabinet in the middle of the front room because we were going to hang my floral quilt on the wall today before the shop opened. She started giving us instructions and we obeyed, hoping to do it in a timely manner.

"You must allow me to tell you, Miss Anne, that this is quite lovely here," Jean admired, with her hands together in praise. "It really fancies an English garden."

"What a conversation piece, Anne!" Sally added. "This whole town will know about those basement quilters. Julia even put the sleeve on the back when she knew how we were going to hang it."

"I must remember to thank her," I agreed, as I also admired the handiwork. "Why don't we have Kevin drop off a nice little basket of fall flowers for her? Any table can use flowers this time of year."

"Will do, Miss Anne. She will love it so," responded Jean. "We put your mother's table arrangement in the fridge yesterday, so don't forget."

When we unlocked the door, an attractive and rather sexy young woman approached the counter and asked to see me. She was dressed in the latest cutting-edge clothing that I barely remembered from my youth. Her hair was in a spiky style that I always admired and never had the nerve to wear.

I left my computer for a visit that piqued my interest.

"Hi, Mrs. Dickson. I'm Abbey Kaufman," she announced. "I met your husband last week and he said you were looking for some part-time help in floral designing. I worked for a boutique in New York, but haven't found work since I moved here, so I thought I'd see if I could apply. I also paint canvases but you sure can't do that to pay bills." She was strikingly different. I was curious about her.

"Well, come on back to my desk and I'll have you fill out our form," I hastily offered. "So, where did you meet my husband?" Hmmm...

"Well, maybe I shouldn't have mentioned that," she blushed. "I'm working part-time tending bar at the Q and I overheard your husband talking to someone. He's so nice and he was very complimentary of your shop. My job at the Q has ended now, as I was just filling in for someone."

She took the form and went to the counter to fill it out. She was very beautiful in a strange way, almost too beautiful and unique to be working in a flower shop. It was hard to concentrate on her background of floral designing experience as my eyes took in her make-up, odd accessories, and multiple ear piercings. After taking her application, I told her I would read her bio and then call her if I thought she'd be a good fit for us. When she went out the door, Kevin came in the door and responded boldly as any man would do. We all laughed. Sally commented about how more cleavage around the place would get us more business. I didn't even want to think about how she may have flirted with my husband at a bar.

Sam called to remind me of his mother arriving at the airport that evening. I was dreading the visit, as I really didn't know her well and our house wasn't quite the way I wanted it to be for houseguests. She would be sleeping in the guest room that contained my antique bedroom set from home. I had prepared the room the night before and wanted to bring home fresh flowers to place on her bedside table.

Sam decided that we would have dinner at Donna's Tea Room tonight because she seemed to enjoy it so much from her earlier visits. He also knew today would be terribly busy with Thanksgiving Day just two days away. He said he would entertain her tomorrow and do any household chores in preparation for the big day.

"Hello, gals," Mother greeted as she entered the shop. "I just came to check if there was anything else you needed for the dinner." I left my customer to browse around on her own and greeted Mother with a kiss.

"Just be there, Mother," I begged. "You know this is the first important meal I have done since we were married. I've gone over the menu with you and I think I'm okay, but I'm nervous. Remember, you need to help me make the gravy." She grinned with approval.

"Amanda called and she and William want to bring something so I suggested champagne since we had the food covered," Mother explained. "I told them it wasn't necessary, but I think it will make them feel more like family if we let them contribute."

"How is Aunt Mary doing?" I asked.

"They are going to see Mary on their way here. Amanda said Mary's breathing is getting worse and worse. Aunt Julia and I are going to see her next week. Would you like to go with us?"

"Yes, I would, most definitely," I nodded my head.

"Julia and I found two quilts from Grandmother that we are going to give Amanda and William and I want Mary to know that," Mother revealed.

"That's great," I found myself thinking somber thoughts of her joining my Aunt Marie in heaven. Aunt Marie and Grandmother Davis were the big quilters in the family. They made enough quilts to go around to everyone!

"Here's the nice big tablecloth from my mother-in-law Grandmother Brown," Mother said as she handed me the hanger that contained the cream linen and lace tablecloth. "It is so huge, but perfect for that long table of yours. You can just keep it, for it's even a bit big for my table at home. It's just in the closet hanging there."

Gayle then came in the door and wanted to know if we all knew about the break-in at the spice shop. This kept Mother there another half hour with all her questions. I kept working in between words of warning from Mother.

"Have you let Sam know this happened?" Mother asked, with a frightened look on her face.

"I will tonight," I assured her. "I am too busy and there's nothing to be done. The police have all the information."

"Don't forget, next week is the Austen Club, Miss Sylvia," Jean reminded everyone. "It's *Sense and Sensibility* if you recall."

"They are expecting snow next week," Mother warned. "It's supposed to be a pretty bad storm."

"Does this mean Mrs. Dickson could get snowed in here?" I asked in jest.

It got a good laugh from everyone but they all knew my underlying concern.

"I'm sure things will be fine," I said with hope in my voice.

"Actually, I would like to know her better and find out more about Sam as a young boy. I'm sure he was perfect, just like me, right Mother?"

"Yes Anne," she said with a grin, "as perfect as any spoiled only child could be!" Hmmm...

CHAPTER 33

I met Sam and Mrs. Dickson at the restaurant and she truly seemed pleased to be here. Her flight was satisfactory but she admitted she was very tired from the day. She explained what the rest of her family was doing tomorrow and was sorry they were not with her.

"You will love spending a little time here in Colebridge and catching up with that son of yours," I said to comfort her.

"He sounds mighty busy if you ask me," she said with some sarcasm. "I hate he has to be the one to take off work and cook a turkey, too." Hmmm, I had to digest that sentence to make sure I was hearing it in the correct sense.

"Mother, I told you I have some vacation days coming and besides, I have missed you," Sam said quickly, to cover the overtones. "This is one of Anne's busiest times in the shop, plus you know how much I love to cook. Sylvia will be coming over early as well to do a few things."

"Why would that be necessary if I'm there?" she asked, looking only at Sam.

"It isn't necessary, but this is our first big dinner and everyone wants to help in any way they can," he said, not looking my way or wanting to feel the light kick to his leg under the table.

"The two of you seemed to enjoy each other's company, so you must do that very thing and let Sam and I entertain you," I nicely explained.

Our dinner could not be over fast enough and I too was so tired I could hardly talk. I kept thinking about getting the table set when I got home so that tomorrow could be all about the food.

We both carried her things up the stairs to the finished guest room and said we'd be happy to make her tea if she wanted to join us in the study downstairs. She gave the room an once-over look.

"I think I need to get some rest, but you may want to remove these flowers sitting here," she quickly observed. "I'm allergic to these lilies, I can tell you that. They are lovely but, if you don't mind, I can't be sleeping with these in the same room."

"Since when did you become allergic, Mother?" asked Sam, picking up the vase.

"This past spring, I'm afraid," she stated without wanting to continue the topic.

"Is there anything else we can bring you before we say good night, Helen?" I said, hoping the answer would be no. "There is bottled water on your nightstand and some toiletries if you forgot anything."

"My goodness, this is just like a hotel," she reflected. Was this a compliment, I wondered?

We both kissed her good night and I went straight to the dining room to begin spreading out the lace tablecloth. Sam joined me from the kitchen where he had put the beautiful bouquet of lilies. He came up from behind me and put his arms around me in consolation.

"You are a gem, my sweet. I'm sorry that Mother was so insensitive to your thoughtfulness. She can be this way with my sisters, too, but I am the only son and probably her favorite, so I can do no wrong."

I smiled and kept working in silence for a time. Before I went into the study to kiss Sam good night, I went to the kitchen to make sure the flowers were not thrown away. Grandmother Davis would surely respond to such a practice. I placed them in the center of the kitchen table in hopes it would keep her out of the kitchen for tomorrow's feast.

Mother arrived promptly the next morning. Sam and I were quietly moving around, having our coffee. So far, we had not heard a peep out of Helen. Mother raved about the beautiful table setting and concurred that Emily Post would've been quite pleased. I looked at the floral centerpiece and, sure enough, there were a few lilies in the arrangement. I carefully removed them and added them to the bouquet in the kitchen. Sam had put the turkey in the oven and within the half hour, aromas were abounding around the room. Mother was layering the green bean casserole when Helen joined us in the kitchen. She and Mother greeted each other politely and I immediately got Helen a cup of tea instead of coffee, which I thought was her practice.

"Thanks Anne, but in the morning, I take to my coffee," she said, placing herself down right smack in front of the bouquet of lilies.

"I have some delicious muffins I just got out of the oven, Mother," Sam offered proudly. She helped herself and thanked him graciously.

"They are delicious," chimed Mother. "I would have another, but don't want to spoil my appetite for this special meal we are about to experience."

"Well, it appears my help isn't needed," Helen said as she now discovered the bouquet of lilies.

"Oh Helen, I am being careless. Let me move these flowers," I said, picking them up to walk them to the sun porch. "I don't think it's too cool out here for them."

Mother was confused with the activity, but knew better than to extend the conversation. Sam invited his mother around the house to see where he had done some improvements, as well as showing her the new security system. He knew there were already too many cooks in the kitchen.

I barely had finished changing clothes when I heard the first guest arrive. When I heard giggles and funny sounds, I knew it must be Sue and Mia. I came downstairs to notice she had brought a high chair for Mia.

"I have an extra chair so I thought we could just keep this one here for her," she offered, after she gave me a kiss on the cheek.

I couldn't resist a forced hug and kiss from Mia. When she saw Sam get down to her level, she ran to him with open arms.

"Sam's always had a special way with children," bragged Helen, as she watched the two of them. "Soon he will have little ones of his own running through this big house, and then we'll see how well he does." Hmmm, we'll see about that, I thought.

No one had to respond because in the door came Amanda and William. Mother made their introductions to Helen so I was relieved of that duty. Aunt Julia and Sarah were the last to arrive. Sarah was upset with her mother about something but I pretended I didn't notice anything.

Sarah followed me in the kitchen to get some drinks and sat down with a pout on her face.

"I wanted to invite my dad," Sarah said, with a soft voice so only I could hear. "I know you wouldn't have minded. I don't think he had a place to go, and he loves all you guys."

"Oh Sarah, you're right," I said, joining her at the table. "Sam and I would have loved the idea, but your mother would have been pretty upset if we did. You see, your mother is the one on this side of the family, so we have to consider her feelings. I bet anything he has been invited to Thanksgiving dinner somewhere."

Sam checked the turkey and placed it on the counter to sit awhile and Mother was already working on the gravy.

"Sarah, would you mind filling the water glasses?" I asked, trying to get her mind off things. "I need to be getting the vegetables ready for the table."

William walked into the kitchen and admired all of the latest kitchen décor.

"I envy this kitchen," he said with admiration as he looked around. "I love to cook. By the way, I'll be happy to pour the wine you have placed on the sideboard."

"That would be a great help," said Sam. "I think I'll carve this at the table, Anne. Everyone always enjoys seeing the big brown turkey before it's fed to the wolves."

"Great idea. It smells heavenly," I said, looking at Sam with such admiration.

"I think we have it all together, Anne," Mother said as she removed her apron.

"You gather your guests around the table. Mia is already in her high chair waiting to chew on something."

I did just as she suggested and the crowd gathered without hesitation. They all looked for their place cards and stood behind their chairs until the host had taken his place behind the roasted turkey. I mentally patted myself on the back for pulling this perfect Kodak moment together in my own home at 333 Lincoln.

CHAPTER 34

To my surprise, Sam asked everyone to join hands for grace. Sue made sure to include Mia's little hands, which connected Sue with one hand and my mother on the other.

"May God bless this food, our home, and all the family within this room," Sam prayed aloud. "Bless also those who are not with us today. We are truly thankful, and in God's name, we say Amen." I had chills running up and down my spine with pride and love. Then I silently thanked the Lord above in my own special way.

As soon as we were seated, chatter impulsively developed around the table. Sam began carving the turkey and then an unexpected toast started our meal.

"I'd like to make a toast to Sam and Anne Dickson. They not only opened their lovely home to this festive meal, but accepted Amanda and me into this loving family, which just a year ago, we didn't know we had," William said with such grace.

"Hear ye!" was cheered by all. With that said, I noticed tears well up in my mother's eyes as well as Amanda's. Helen was completely in the dark regarding the comment and was sure to question Sam as soon as she could about William's toast. Sam and I looked at each other in complete harmony. He winked at me as he passed me my plate of turkey slices. I could hardly eat a bite as I watched everyone devour the dishes passed around to them. I wanted to be the hostess to see that everyone had what they wanted. I had forgotten to put butter on the table for the rolls and we were in need of more water, so when I went to the refrigerator to grab what I needed, I noticed a pitcher of lemonade that had not been there earlier. I grinned and took out the pitcher to show my love and appreciation on this festive occasion. This was truly becoming Grandmother's trademark for celebration.

When I walked into the dining room, Mother and Aunt Julia had to take a second look when I asked if anyone preferred lemonade. Now I wish I had left the lilies in the table arrangement. As I walked around the table to see if anyone needed anything, I picked up bits and pieces of conversation. Sam was telling Mother that the Barristers had gone back to Boston for the holiday and that Uncle Jim had been invited to his sister's house for Thanksgiving. Mia was ready for dessert and starting to squirm out of her chair. Helen continued bragging to Aunt Julia that I was lucky to have Sam with all his talents to use in the home. I could hear Aunt Julia try to defend me without success. Amanda was sharing with Mother that Aunt Mary had sent her love to everyone, but was completely bedridden now.

When I started to clear some of the dishes, Mother immediately rose to help. When we arrived at the kitchen sink together, she asked me if Jean and Sally had a place to go today.

"Yes," I answered as Sue joined us. "Sally was going with Paige to her parents' home and Jean and Al were joining their next-door neighbors."

"I think Paige has been good for Sally. She said at quilting one afternoon that Paige was always trying to fix her up. She also said that Paige was from a very wealthy family in St. Louis. Did you know that?"

"No," I answered. "Sally shares very little of her personal life around me. I know more about Jean and Al than her."

"I think William may have a girlfriend, according to something Amanda said," Mother added.

"Well, I sure look forward to bringing someone special to our family dinners one day," Sue said as a tease.

"You will, you will," said Mother who gave her a quick squeeze. "Will you each take a dessert and place it on the buffet? I'll bring the coffee."

The compliments were flowing on the delicious meal, with the exception of Helen, of course. She avoided all of the three dessert choices with some health explanation about each of them. She never left Sam's presence for one moment. She looked the other way when Sam grabbed me for a quick kiss as he took a sample of each of the desserts. The largest hurdle was over, I told myself. We took our desserts into our partially furnished living room and Sam brought in a couple of chairs from the dining room. The fireplace provided just the right amount of warmth as the day had become colder and cloudy. Mia and Sarah were in front of the TV in the study.

"I tried to think of a guest for you this Thanksgiving,

Aunt Julia." I teased with her as she sat next to me on the love seat. "Had you and Uncle Jim not brought Sam to Thanksgiving dinner last year, I wouldn't have this husband today."

"I suggest you never consider that act of mercy, Anne," she responded softly so no one else could hear. "The last thing I need right now is another man in my life. I have to admit, I envy you right now. Sam is many things that Jim was not and never would be. I don't think there are many Sams in this world. By the way, will you be at the Austen meeting this week?"

"Yes," I answered with a smirk. "Don't change the subject on me. Are you really doing okay?"

"Nothing a little wine every night can't cure," she joked, lifting a glass of wine she was still nursing from the dinner table. I didn't want to analyze that comment right now. Hmmm...

CHAPTER 35

The next morning, I was in no hurry to start the day. I knew the shop would be slow after the holiday, and with Helen visiting, I chose to take the day off. There were very few mornings that I woke up next to Sam. He was an early riser and worked his best in the morning. He usually started the coffee just as my mother had done for me all my adult life. If Helen were not in our schedule, I would take my walk and then do some clean-up work outdoors. With the talk of a storm coming, I wanted to make sure certain plants were covered and that I had some heat coming into the potting shed. When I joined Sam downstairs, he was reading the paper in the sunroom. It wasn't heated, but the morning sun worked miracles and the bouquet of lilies was just as beautiful as when I put it there. I made a small egg casserole ahead of time that I had memorized from watching Mother make it so often. I knew Sam was looking forward to having some and, if I got lucky, Helen would approve and join us.

I joined Sam in the sunroom by pushing the paper aside and sitting on his lap to kiss him good morning.

"Job well done yesterday, Annie," he whispered as if his mother might be coming in the door. "I really like Amanda and William. They seem to really want to be a part of your family."

"Our family," I corrected. "I will try to include them when I can. I have a question for you, by the way. Do you remember meeting a barmaid at the Q by the name of Abbey, by chance?" He chuckled. "She's pretty striking and she obviously felt comfortable enough to come to the shop to ask me for a job."

"Now that you say a job, yes, I remember," he recalled. "Jim and I were making small talk and I think she said she just moved here from New York. We asked what she did, if I remember correctly. Anyway, she said she did floral designing for a boutique. That's when I told her I was married to one of those flower people. Oh I think I said *happily* married." We both couldn't help but laugh at the thought.

"Well, she did come in, and I have to say, she made an impression on all of us, at least by the way she was dressed," I described. "She's pretty young, but she's had some college and retail experience. I actually liked her, but I'm not sure she would fit in, if you know what I mean."

"You want some management advice here as I try to wear your hat?" Sam asked as he got up to get more coffee.

"Yes, yes I do," I eagerly answered.

"In the creative business that you're in, do you really want everyone to be cloned in that shop? She is young and a bit crazy, perhaps, but looking to the future, don't you need that component to your kind of business? You can give her a trial period to judge her flower and people skills, and, if it doesn't work, you move on."

"Why are you so darn smart?" I responded with admiration. "I'm so glad to hear you say that because when I saw her, I thought how creative and bold she made her appearance. You and Uncle Jim weren't hitting on her, were you?"

He was ready to smack me on my rear end with the newspaper when Helen joined us in the den. She gave us an odd look, but did not comment.

"I smell something really good in that kitchen," she said pleasantly.

"It's a casserole that's just about done so I hope you have an appetite," I happily explained.

"Sam, didn't you do enough? I could still eat some of those great muffins you had yesterday."

"Well, Mother, I didn't have anything to do with breakfast. Anne made this for us," he bragged as I turned away to not show my true response. "She said Sylvia have made this recipe for years. Is it ready, Anne?"

Helen was nice enough to accommodate us with the casserole and fresh fruit. She didn't apologize for her incorrect comment, but she did provide me with a compliment or two as she was eating. I asked her what she would like to do today, and she did not respond with any suggestions; so I confessed I wanted to walk off some calories from the day before if she didn't mind.

"Heavens no, Anne, you go right ahead with your plans," she offered. "I'll join Sam with the newspaper and TV. If you don't mind, I'll have to remove the lilies on this table. By the way, I wondered the other day if the fresh lilies are still appearing on the grave of Mr. Taylor. I'll never forget that sight on my last visit. I remember you explaining that his dead mistress might be the source."

"Yes, the lilies still appear just as they have here at 333 Lincoln," I said bravely, hoping to scare her. "The lemonade is also a frequent gift from her. I'm glad you enjoyed some of that yesterday."

Her look was ghastly and she wasn't sure if I was teasing or not. Before the conversation could go any further, Sam was yelling from the sunroom.

"Anne, Anne, come quickly!" Sam shouted, pointing to the TV. "Listen. Listen to this report."

The visual was police cars in front of some house and the reporter was saying they couldn't reveal the names of the deceased until the relatives were notified. The woman reporter went on to say the place was in shambles, indicating a fight, which she thought involved drugs, according to the police.

"Sam, I don't understand," I said, quite puzzled. "Do you know who she is talking about?" Helen now joined us as we watched for further information.

"I think we do know, Anne," Sam said with fear in his voice. "I think this is Steve. They said it was a brother and a sister. The sister was shot and then the brother who shot her committed suicide. Didn't Officer Wilson tell you he was on the prowl for drugs?"

I couldn't speak. Chills were taking over my body. I sat on the floor to stare into the screen. The reporter said they would have more details on the evening news and then she was gone, just like that. No one knew what to say. Helen knew this was all mysterious but, to her credit, she just stared at us for an explanation. I broke down in tears and ran up the stairs, leaving Sam to explain.

Our landline phone rang as soon as I shut the bedroom door. It was Kevin. Sam and I both answered the phone at the same time.

"Did you hear, Anne?" Kevin's shaky voice said. I couldn't speak.

"Hey, Kevin. Anne and I are both on the line, and yes, we heard," Sam explained with sadness. "What else can you tell us? It was Steve, right?"

"Yeah," he said much more calmly. "My friend Erik called me and said he knew that was his sister's house because he dropped him off there one time. Steve must have really been high to do that to his sister."

"Drugs can make you pretty desperate," Sam responded.

"Kevin, when you get to the shop, call me if you hear anything else," I finally responded. "If Officer Wilson tries to reach me there, tell him I am at home, will you?"

"Sure, Anne," he said with comforting tones. "You don't have to be afraid anymore. None of us has to be afraid of this guy anymore. This is justice served, if you ask me. Take care."

No, it wasn't justice for his poor sister who tried to help him. I wondered if I would have done something differently, then the two of them would still be alive and Steve alone could pay the price for his behavior. Sam then came into the room and I broke down in tears in his arms. I think I had refused to be intimidated by this person. I didn't have time to be afraid and didn't want to admit I was in danger. Now I learned he had a gun. I wondered if he was the one who broke into the spice shop for cash. Was it Steve who tried to break into my shop? Did this all start with me letting him go from a job that he really wanted? Was he a bad guy before I hired him? I was indeed the person he hated as he left his notes through the mail slot. Somehow I couldn't stop crying. I'm sure he had a mother or some family that would be terribly heartbroken by now.

Sam let me cry until I was silent. He knew there were no words. There was little to feel good about other than that my fear of Steve in my life was now over. This would forever be in my mind and I wanted God to know I had forgiven this sick man for any disruptions in my life. I left Sam to explain it to his mother, who was silenced in the wonder of it all.

CHAPTER 36

A good time later, I went outdoors to clear my head, as well as be productive. I wanted to be alone with things that were close to God, like the innocence of plants that grew without complaint. I took in the cooler temperatures that told me our first snow of the season might be at our doorstep. I released my energy by sweeping up the leaf-covered potting shed and then took one of the tulip bulb packages outdoors to plant about the beds for spring color. I got down on my knees and pushed the dirt harder than usual with my handy tulip spade. The ground was still soft enough to penetrate as deeply as I needed to go. As my energy continued to surge, I dug up the large elephant ear plant with my shovel and placed it in one of my largest clay pots, in hopes it would survive my sparsely heated shed during the coming winter. When I closed the door to the shed, the lights flickered on and off as they had once before, telling me somehow that I wasn't alone.

169

I sat on the stool, acknowledged her presence, and started crying all over again. Why was I feeling like I had been partly responsible for what had just happened to this mentally disturbed person? The lights stood still and I felt the need to act like the big girl who owned and operated the flower shop on Main Street.

I walked in the house and found Sam alone in the study.

"Feel any better, Annie?" Sam asked in his loving voice.

"Yes, much," I said putting my arms around his neck. "I'm sorry I reacted so poorly."

"Well, we did get that call from Officer Wilson and he said there's no hurry for him to get what more information he needs," explained Sam. "He'll call you early next week sometime."

"Did he tell you any more details?" I asked, not sure I really wanted to know.

"It was drug related, just like they said," he repeated. "They think the argument started when she wouldn't give him money for drugs or she didn't have it to give."

Helen now came in the room and said that she was sorry for everyone concerned. Somehow, I felt she meant it. She knew this was most personal to Sam and me.

"I ordered some pizza to be delivered," Sam announced to me. "Does that sound good?"

"Yes, I'm starved," I remarked, thinking about it. "I worked up an appetite out there, but I feel better having done some of the work with the bad weather coming and all."

"Speaking of the weather, are those snowflakes I see coming down out there?" Helen said as she went to the window. "I hope I can still fly out in the morning."

I turned to go into the kitchen to wash my hands, and

promised myself I would fly her home tomorrow myself if I had to. The tiny flakes seemed to disappear when they hit the ground.

After a full stomach and exhaustion from crying and digging, I said good night to Helen and Sam joined me in turning in early for the night. I showered and then realized that the falling snow was now accumulating on the lawn, hedges, and driveway. Our first winter in our home was so comforting. I crawled in bed beside my man who was nearly asleep. I had much to be thankful for and life was indeed very good, despite the horrid news that day.

Sam and Helen left early for the airport without me hearing them. I really had a deep night's worth of sleep. I put on my robe and called Sally from the bedside table phone.

"How's the weather over there?" I asked, thinking of her steep driveway.

"I'm good. The roads are fine," she described. "I'll open the shop, so don't break your neck getting in. Kevin called last night and told me about Steve. Paige and I were at the movies, so I missed the news coverage."

"Do me a favor and fill Jean in before I get there," I requested. "I really don't like talking about all of this and I'm sure Nick and whoever else from the street will all be buzzing about that today."

"Not to worry, Anne," she said with understanding.

"I'm going to call Abbey Kaufman and see if she can come in today or tomorrow on a trial basis," I said, not knowing what kind of reaction I would get. "I think we could use some New York creativity to put us a little more on the cutting edge. What do you think?"

"Go for it," she said with some excitement. "We'll just

have to keep Kevin on the road or he'll be all over her in the shop." We laughed.

I dressed and went down to the kitchen where the lilies appeared back on the kitchen table somehow. Next to the bouquet was a handwritten note that read: *Thanks for everything, Anne. You are a lovely hostess and wife who is making my son very happy. Love, Helen.*

CHAPTER 37

I parked in the rear of the shop and hoped that no one would know I was there. Abbey said she could meet me at eleven, so it would give me a little time for some computer work. A bit later, Sally came to my desk after a customer left to tell me several street people had stopped by to see what I thought of the hot story circulating around town. We were too busy, despite the bad weather, for her and Jean to take out time for gossip and I had to get busy on some orders placed for the week ahead. Sam called to check on me. He was very behind on his work with his mother's visit taking so much of his time. He said he might be working late. I was hoping I could block out the Steve story as much as possible and get on with my life. It was not easy to do so, as I would never, never forget the outcome and wonder whether I could have changed anything.

Abbey walked in with an additional color of bright red in her strikingly black hair. Her short polka dot skirt and high boots were accented with a bright yellow sweater that still allowed a slight cleavage. A hint of a tattoo here and there was an additional accessory that I hadn't noticed earlier. Jean sent her back to my desk. She was extremely pleased with my phone call and thanked me over and over.

"I'd like you to first learn the cash register," I instructed. "The other skills can be learned as we can fit them into the schedule, but in case we need you to help us immediately, you'll know what to do to take sales. You must remember, it's the customer at the register that deserves our first attention. Then I'd like you to design some things for the cooler so I have a sense of what you design best and see if I think we have a market for such arrangements. I know you'll think outside the box, and I'm counting on your taking us to a level of fun and more unique arrangements. If there is a product you feel we should carry to achieve that, just let me know."

"Super, Anne, if I may call you that," Abbey responded politely. "Don't worry about the register. I think I have worked almost every kind there is. I must tell you that when I arrived in Colebridge, I walked Main Street like everyone else and I really thought your unique vases and window displays were very cool. You didn't seem to use the ordinary, if you know what I mean. I dig that! I would love to live in one of these apartments on the street. If you ever hear of any for rent, would you let me know?"

"Sure, I think I could send you to a few of the landlords I know," I said happily. "I think it would be cool to live on the street as well. I don't know if you're a walker, but the trail along the river and window shopping on the street are pretty unique experiences in Colebridge."

"Miss Anne, the weather is a bit more frightening. Have you looked out?" Jean said nervously. "We've had a great purse today considering the bloody snow! With your kindness, I'd like to cut out a tad early since it has slowed a bit here in the shop."

"Absolutely, Jean," I agreed. "Are you okay to drive, or will Al come and get you?"

"Ta-ta," she quickly responded. "The chap is no better at this than me so I'll make a go if it."

The snow was piling up very quickly and when I looked outdoors, there didn't seem to be a shop open or a car on the street. I decided we needed to close as well. I was grateful no one was expecting a delivery until tomorrow. After I said the good-byes and locked the door, I called Kevin to make sure that regardless of the weather, he needed to show up by nine the next day. When I thought about venturing home myself, I panicked just thinking of the steep drive up to 333 Lincoln. What did the Taylors do in the past? Should I take advantage of being a wife and call my husband for some advice? What would I have done without a husband? The phone then startled my thoughts and it was Mother, who was safely home on Melrose Street but was worried about her daughter at the shop. The first thing out of her mouth was to wonder if I could I make it up the hill to our house. Mothers would always be mothers!

"I'm worried about that, too," I confessed. "I hate to bother Sam. He is so busy at work."

"Why don't you come on over here and have Sam pick you up here?" Mother suggested. "I have some nice vegetable soup that I'd love to share with you. Mr. Carter has cleared the driveway more than once today."

"Thanks so much," I said, despite how comforting it all sounded. "I'm going to leave a message for Sam to pick me up here when he leaves work, I think. I have so much work to do and it's nice to have some peace and quiet. By the way, I did hire Abbey today, but then I let everyone go home early because of the weather. I'm anxious to see what she can do. I like her!"

"Good, Anne," she said with satisfaction. "You are going to need her going into the Christmas season. Just think, your first Christmas at 333 Lincoln is just around the corner."

"Tell me about it," I responded. "Sally started playing Christmas music in the shop already today. I want a really, really big tree in that entry hall at the house. I have pictured that since the first day I saw the place. Then I'll have one in the living room and study. I don't know if I want live ones or not. Sam will probably have an opinion on that, right?" She laughed and agreed with me. "Thanks for not bringing up the Steve story, Mother."

"It's over and done with," she said softly. "Nancy called me the other day for more details, not wanting to bother you. She's worried about you. She did say they had him and his sister at the funeral home and how sad it all was."

With that horrific picture, I hung up with my good-byes. I was reminded that funeral homes were for everyone, good or bad, and that people were hurting in all directions. I shook the thought out of my mind as soon as I could by checking the stock in the cooler and rearranging some empty spots on the display counter. One of the magnificent perks of owning a flower shop was no matter what was going on in the outside world, my world was alive and beautiful here at Brown's Botanical Flower Shop. I always thought of plants as little lives in a pot, just like books were like minds on a shelf. Hmmm...

CHAPTER 38

Sam and I made a safe trip home, thanks to Martingale's snow removal service. Sam had them swing by and do our drive earlier that day. We both were tired and stressed as we settled in with a glass of merlot in the study. Sam confessed he had been having some light chest pains throughout the day. He had been pleased with the medication that had been prescribed and bragged about how he didn't have any pains until today, so he wasn't very concerned.

"What is going on Sam? Is it work?" I asked, with my heart beating faster. "You don't need any of this merlot with that medication." I removed the glass that was placed next to him.

"I have been under a lot of stress, Anne," he admitted, taking in a deep breath. "I don't like to bring my work home because I need a break from it all."

"This home should be more than just a happy place, Sam,"

I said, looking straight into his eyes. "We need a safe place where we both can come together to talk and console each other when we need to about problems as well as joys. I certainly want that, don't you?"

"Okay, Anne," he said with a long pause and then a deep breath. "We're going to be laying off a good number of employees, including some at the administrative level. I'm part of the staff that will determine who can stay and who has to go."

"That's an awful burden, Sam," I answered with sympathy. "When does this have to be done?"

"Soon, but it gets worse, Anne," he went on. "One of the persons on the list is Jim. His performance has really dropped since his divorce and he doesn't seem the least bit disturbed about it. I have tried to drop a few hints, but you know Jim."

"Oh, my word! Is it for sure?"

"It appears to be," Sam was now pacing the room. "He'll probably be told next week. I don't know whether to tell him ahead of time or just let the process work."

"I know how much we both care for him. Would it be better if he were told, so he could resign?"

"He might prefer it, but his benefits would be shattered." Sam was now looking paler and paler.

"Is he still seeing Brenda?" I queried, feeling very brave.

"Not real sure, but that little fling hasn't been helpful to his situation."

"I think you have to reverse the situation and think about what you would want if Uncle Jim knew something about your future."

"I did that and I don't like my results." Sam was now

sitting next to me. "I would want to know what was coming down the pike and I would expect my best friend to be honest and helpful to me handling the situation."

"There's your answer. I think you'll feel better overall if you prepare him. He's not going to hold the decision against you, I know that much."

"Oh, what makes you think so?"

"For one thing, he knows all the players at work. He will sense it's not all your fault and by coming to him ahead of time, you are showing respect and feelings for him. You'll know when the time is right to take him aside. He knows what a great and honest person you are and that it was hard for you to come forward."

"I wouldn't say anything to Julia," Sam warned, as he paced the floor once more. "He's going to have to work all that out himself and you shouldn't get involved."

"I don't think you can ask that of me, Sam," I replied, wanting to be firm. "I'm not going to bring this up. That isn't my job, but I will be there for Aunt Julia and Sarah if they need me. They are family and it will impact them."

"You're right, I guess," he concurred. "I just didn't want you to be put in the middle of a work decision that you had no control of, that's all. Why do things like this always happen right before Christmas?"

We hugged each other for reassurance. We walked to the kitchen to share leftover stir-fry and then called it a night. We both tossed and turned as we watched the hours on the clock tick by. My mind drifted between Sam's recent chest pains and Uncle Jim getting laid off from work. Another fear surfaced as I rolled over. What if Sam lost his best friend through this ordeal? Help us, dear Lord, I repeated in my mind.

The morning finally came, despite my worn out body and soul. Sam was absent from his pillow as he was most mornings when I awoke. He was reading the paper when I came down the stairs.

"Your car is probably snowed in at the shop," he noted as he gave me a kiss on my cheek. "Will Kevin have time to shovel you out or do you want me to help you?"

"I'll be fine," I reassured him. "Kevin has deliveries this morning, but when he gets back, he can take care of it or I'll do it myself."

"Okay, Miss Independent." He gave me a friendly wink. "Can you be ready to leave with me in about fifteen minutes?"

"Sure, just let me eat some cereal," I bargained, pouring milk over my Cheerios.

The sound of the snow removal was now visiting again outdoors. Sam hurried to put on his coat to join them and give them additional instructions. I looked at the lilies still staying fresh on my kitchen table as I munched away on my cereal. I thought of the Taylors eating in this very kitchen. Then I thought of the spiritual presence of Grandmother Davis, the mistress, sitting at this table in the very same room.

CHAPTER 39

There was a good side and a bad side to being the first one to arrive at the shop each day. I was facing the bad side this morning. After I unlocked the front door, I got a broom and shovel to tidy up the sidewalk, put down more salt, and swept off the windowpanes. As I peered in the frosted windows, the fresh colors of green and red peered out the windows as a sign of the festive holiday to come. Our flower boxes were now filled with cabbages, ivy, and baby cedar trees that we decorated with white lights and red bows each year. I loved Christmas! It was a profitable season for the shop, and with Abbey on board to help, I was exceedingly hopeful. Before I came in from the freezing cold, I greeted Gayle and Diane from the shop next door. Then I saw Abbey pull up behind my car on the street. Everyone typically parked in our spaces behind the shop, but in bad weather it wasn't always a good idea, because of the slanted pavement. They joined other shop owners as they parked on the street, in hopes the snow plow would not bury them during the day. The unfortunate result was no room for brave customers who tried to park in front of their desired shop.

We both entered the shop nearly frozen and Abbey took her coat off to reveal another entertaining outfit. There was no sign of a winter wardrobe in her scanty and brightly colored ensemble.

"I brought some photos from my boutique in New York if you'd like to see some of my work," she bragged. "Of course, we had a different clientele than here at your shop, but perhaps we could tweak some of these ideas into surprises of color and joy for Brown's Botanical!" We both had to laugh at the thought.

"I like that. Surprises of color and joy," I repeated. "Most of what we do for folks is a surprise and usually joyful, except for funerals, of course. Thanks so much for bringing these. May I keep them for a while to analyze what I'm looking at?"

"No problem," she said as she went back to her project from the day before. "Is it okay if I use some of this floral spray paint on a container if I need to?"

"Sure, I think we have done that before, so just go out back to make sure it doesn't affect anything else."

Jean and Sally were followed in by Kevin; they all had chosen to park in the rear of the shop. They were joking around as they often did. Jean was already wound up for the Austen Club later this evening at her house. They had an early start discussing *Sense and Sensibility,* the book chosen for the evening's discussion.

I gave Kevin his list of deliveries and sent him on his way. He had become a more serious guy around me after the Steve incident. I know he felt badly about ever introducing him to me and I felt guilty about how I handled things.

"Will you be joining us this evening, Miss Anne?" Jean asked politely.

"I really want to, Jean, and I know Mother will be counting on me, but I won't say for sure until I hear from my husband."

"What am I hearing?" said Sally in a teasing manor. "Are you waiting to get permission from your husband? Is that what I heard?" We all laughed, knowing she was trying to get a rise out of me.

"It's not like that, you guys, but I'm really worried about him," I shared as they all got quiet. "He's under a lot of stress at work and is having chest pains again. It's hard for me to think of anything else right now. To be honest with you, if he's all right, I think it would be good for me to get my mind off of everything."

The phone started ringing on a regular basis with orders from the unexpected death of a long-time Colebridge resident who had done a great deal for the non-profits in our community. I didn't know him personally, but knew his money had achieved many good things. I told Abbey to get right on some of the requests and put her experimental designs on hold.

"Anne, Sally said this gentleman was also quite the pianist," Abbey repeated. "Would it be okay to incorporate some of this musical ribbon and do a black and white arrangement on this order? They didn't specify what they wanted."

"I like it, Abbey, but just don't get too far out with it," I warned.

"His wife would love it, I think," added Sally.

Mother was the next phone call to answer and I told her I would have to wait until the afternoon to know whether I could pick her up or not for the Austen Club. I encouraged her to go, regardless of my schedule. I could feel the let down in her voice as I explained. I didn't want it to be a habit of putting her off with excuses. I knew she would be looking forward to each and every time we could be together and I knew how much she must miss me bopping down to the kitchen each morning to get the latest news and plans for my day.

It was now after two in the afternoon and I hadn't heard a peep from Sam. I didn't want to be overly protective regarding his situation, but I wanted some reassurance from him that all was well. Aunt Julia stopped by to pick up an arrangement for one of her neighbors who had done some nice repair work for her on the weekend. She said she had lunch at Charley's and saw Sam and Uncle Jim sitting at the bar together.

"They're two peas in a pod," she joked. "Sarah is going away skiing with Jim for the weekend. She's so excited. We went as a family about five years ago and she still talks about it like it was yesterday."

"Wow, that is pretty cool," I added with excitement. "He's probably going to do more with her now than if you were all together under one roof."

"My only concern is that there will be some other hitches to this, like some blonde bombshell waiting there who's like Brenda," she divulged quietly so the others could not hear.

"Aunt Julia, he wouldn't," I said with fear in my voice.

"I don't put anything past him, Anne," she quipped. "Will

you be going to the Austen Club tonight? Sarah always looks forward to it and it's really good for her to do all this reading. I really love my time with Mia."

"As of now, I will likely be there." I had to cut her off to help a customer.

"Thanks for the order, Aunt Julia." She flew out the door. I felt so guilty not saying a word about the extra drama that was to come in their lives.

Why did unfortunate circumstances have to force others to choose sides? If this didn't go well, Sam would be supporting Uncle Jim and I would be supporting Aunt Julia. Then there was poor Sarah in the middle, trying to be loyal to each of them. If Sarah ever learned of Uncle Jim's relationship with Brenda, I fear it would haunt her future with the father she adored.

CHAPTER 40

I felt better going to the club meeting after I heard from Sam. He said he was having a good day and having dinner with an out-of-town client so I didn't feel guilty about my plans. Mother was delighted when I called to tell her I'd be picking her up.

It was good to see Nancy when I walked in the front door. We needed to catch up after her being gone for the holidays. We grabbed our teacups and cookies, which was now my dinner, and sat next to each other in the corner of the room. I wanted to ask her more questions about Steve's funeral, but this was not the place nor the time. Jean was adamant about starting on time and wanted to stay focused during our next discussion.

"*Sense and Sensibility* was Jane Austen's first published novel," began Jean. "Its three volumes appeared in 1811 under the pseudonym '*A Lady*'. The first run was 1,000 copies, and she not only had to pay for it herself, but also had to pay the publisher a commission of the sales. Did everyone get a chance to read it or get a good grip on what it was all about?"

"I frankly found it quite confusing keeping the Dashwood girls separate and who was who," revealed Sue.

"Me too," chimed in Sarah. "I did feel badly for Marianne when John left her, though."

"He did leave her for the wealthy and hateful Miss Grey; but, to his credit, when he learns of Marianne's ill health, he rushes to her side, not wanting her to die hating him," added Nancy.

"So is this a good enough reason for any man to come back, feeling sorry for her and all?" asked Sally. "He didn't want to feel guilty if she died. She's much better off with the Colonel."

"I think Austen did a good job explaining how many of us battle the balance of sense and logic or sensibility in our emotions and how to balance these two extremes," said Paige.

"I say the moral of the story is if Willoughby would have behaved in an honorable fashion, he would have married Marianne and received his inheritance," Jean concluded.

Everyone now joined discussions among themselves, which often happened. It was never my favorite book of Jane's, but it was interesting to hear what everyone took to heart from its contents.

"The next novel is *Mansfield Park*, announced Jean. "Someone can borrow my copy if they need to," Jean offered. "Sally was very kind to bring some of her homemade fudge tonight, so I hope you all have tried it."

"I'm sorry that we never got that cookout arranged," I said to Nancy as we were preparing to leave. "We will spend some time together through the holidays for sure. Sam's mother's visit here for Thanksgiving and other things have sure kept me sidetracked."

"Is everything okay right now?" asked Nancy with concern. "I know this Steve incident has been hard on you two. Was Mrs. Dickson well behaved?"

"My mother-in-law? That is another topic, but all in all, it went pretty well," I explained. "Right now, I am mostly concerned about Sam. He continues to have those chest pains. He has so much stress at work. He has to lay off quite a few employees, and he is really taking it all personally."

"What little I know of Sam, I can understand he would do that," Nancy said with sympathy.

We left, deciding to get together for lunch more often as Mother led me out the door. I could tell she enjoyed the evening and commented on how pleased she was that Sarah was enjoying it as well. My mind was a million miles away when she asked if I had thought about how the Christmas holidays would play out.

I put her off, not wanting to even think about it. I just got Helen Dickson out the door and the thought of her coming back was not a pleasant one.

"I got another call from Amanda, Anne," said Mother, changing the subject. "Mary is not any better. Would you go with me to see her tomorrow or the next day? It's sounding pretty serious."

"Sure, how about day after next? I think Sam goes out of town again. I really worry about him, Mother. He's too young and strong to have all this stress."

"Is he still working out?"

"Not like he used to. His schedule has been very full, especially since he took time off at Thanksgiving. I don't like to nag him. It's a fine line, huh Mother?"

She agreed, laughing as she shared that she had walked that line many times with my father. I kissed her good night and promised I'd see her this week to go visit my Aunt Mary.

CHAPTER 41

S am left for work the next morning in a fairly good mood, which reflected more of his old self. I knew he had put the inevitable aside with matters concerning Uncle Jim's employment.

I firmed up the visit to Aunt Mary's with Mother and scheduled Abbey to help out at the shop for the day. It was a beautiful day and it felt good to get in the car and drive for some time, away from Colebridge. I was looking forward to the next time Sam and I could get away by ourselves again. Mother had been saving up a multitude of topics to discuss with me and I wasn't sure I was listening to half of them as she chatted away.

We finally arrived at the senior home that looked to be very stylish and up to date. When we were shown Aunt Mary's room, there was Amanda to happily greet us. Aunt Mary was hooked up to an oxygen tank, but she lit up when she saw us enter.

"So good to see you both," Amanda said as she took off her mother's breathing mask. "I'll raise Mother's bed a bit so she can see the two of you better."

"I brought you some lovely lilies from my shop, Aunt Mary," I offered, putting them on her bedside table. "I don't know if anyone ever shared with you that your mother loved lilies and your father knew it as well."

"No, for heaven's sake I didn't know that, but I have an unusual fondness for them myself," she added. "You must share as much as you can about her because we all know very little, as you know."

"Mary, our mother always kept things pretty close, if you know what I mean," Mother explained. "You know, back then it wasn't uncommon. She never talked about the past very much at all. She didn't mistreat any of us, but she hid her emotions and affection from us most of the time. I'm just so pleased that Anne found what information she did in those letters in the potting shed quilt."

"Oh, I am too," she said softly. "I hope you all continue to research as much as you can, for William and Amanda's sake. I sure hated to miss your lovely Thanksgiving dinner. Amanda and William enjoyed it all so much. You don't know what it feels like to have found a family connection for us. That young man that you found to marry is so pleasant and quite handsome. I'm very happy for you."

"Thank you, Aunt Mary," I said blushing. "I'm a lucky person, for sure."

"Don't get too busy for him, you hear?" she warned with a smile. "I hear you go nonstop with your business and all."

"I guess I know who you have been talking to," I teased as

I looked at Mother.

"I wish Julia could have come with us today," Mother said, getting closer for Aunt Mary to hear. "She was helping with an event at Sarah's school all day."

"Is she doing okay with the divorce and all, Sylvia?" Aunt Mary asked as she looked toward her breathing mask.

"I can't tell for sure," Mother said with a sad note. "She knew this was coming for a long time." Changing the subject, Mother said, "You know Julia and Mother didn't always see eye to eye. Julia had made a quilt top all by herself and needed some help quilting it, so she brought it to us. Marie had Mother's quilting frame, so that's when we all gathered in the basement to help her quilt it. None of us knew how to quilt, but Marie taught us what we needed to know and now we continue to meet, helping each other with our quilts. We just finished a lovely floral quilt for Anne to put in her flower shop. Mother and Marie would be quite proud. Julia is pleased to have her quilt done because she said Mother always told her that she could never finish anything."

"Oh, it's so good to hear these stories," Aunt Mary said, now having more trouble breathing.

"I think we need to be going, Mother," I suggested. "We don't want to wear her out and I think she could use some of this oxygen."

"Oh no, you all have given her a good deal of joy," said Amanda, smiling at us. "This was so good for her and I hope you all come back real soon."

"We will," I assured her.

"Anne, may I have a word with you alone?" Aunt Mary whispered before she let Amanda put on her mask.

I nodded as Mother said good-bye and left the room

with Amanda.

"You are going to be the matriarch of the family very soon, Anne," she said smiling. "Will you promise me that you will include Amanda and William as much as you can? They have missed out on so much having no family to speak of. I can see there is a real bond here amongst you all and that makes me very happy."

"Not to worry, Aunt Mary," I assured her. "We are growing quite fond of each other and it is a joy for all of us to have found you."

"Sylvia did a good job raising you. Thank you so much," she said, now almost out of breath. I kissed her on the cheek with my misty eyes too blurred to see her.

As I walked down the corridor, I prayed God would take care of her till she joined her extended family in heaven.

Was I ever going to be ready as the matriarch of the family? Hmmm...

CHAPTER 42

As Sam was packing for his next trip, I filled him in on our visit with Aunt Mary. Sam was so organized about everything he did. He turned the sitting room off our bedroom into a place where he kept all his travel items. He was giving me reminders about the alarm system and that he told the plow man to swing by if there was any more bad weather. I told him I was having lunch with Nancy that day and reminded him that we needed to have them over for dinner as soon as possible.

"I'd like to have the house decorated for Christmas, but I don't know how soon that will happen. Nancy is giving me the number for her cleaning lady today. I really thought I could handle this, Sam, because we don't go in half the rooms we have, but they seem to get dirty and dusty anyway." He laughed as he was putting on his suit jacket.

"You will be grateful to have someone in time for the

Christmas holidays," he said with approval.

"Will your mother be willing to come back for Christmas?" I asked, hoping I would get the right answer.

"At the airport, she said she would not be here for Christmas, but was hoping we could get back there for a couple of days. I was thinking we could go for a couple of days between Christmas and New Year. Your business slows down a bit then, am I right?"

"I think that sounds like a plan, honey. I think Mother would like us over for Christmas Eve, and then you and I can start our own tradition on Christmas morning. How does that sound?" I lit up at the very thought.

"I wish it were tomorrow, my sweet," he said, rushing around the room looking for something. "Have you seen my bottle of medication? I had it right here on the end table."

I got up to look around with part of me wanting to get upset. It was not like him to misplace something like this. Then I spotted the bottle on the bathroom countertop.

"Here it is. You just left it here," I said, feeling relieved.

"No, I did not put it there, Anne," he insisted. "Did you do that not wanting me to forget it?"

"No siree!" I quickly responded. "I wouldn't think of doing that and you know it."

"I've got to fly, Anne, so I'll call you tonight, okay?" he said, grabbing me around the waist. "I love you, so stay out of trouble, you hear?"

I saw him to the door to give him a last kiss. As I made my way back up the stairs, I wondered how the pill container got moved. Hmmm...

The next morning, I checked my e-mail from my home laptop as I ate my Cheerios. I thought I'd pick up a Starbucks on the way to the shop.

Once I arrived, there was an e-mail from Amanda saying her mother had gone into pneumonia and that she would keep us posted. She commented again how much our visit meant to her mother. I wondered if this was the beginning of the end for her. Telling me of her request indicated to me she knew she wouldn't be here much longer. I would have to tell Mother today.

I was dressed in business attire since I was going to lunch at the Q with Nancy. It reminded me about some of the organizations I had been neglecting. It was so hard to wear all the hats in a small business. I know many businesses were struggling and there would always be a few turnovers of shops after Christmas. I always felt very lucky to have a business that was built on the community's needs and not just tourists.

Nancy walked in looking like the fashion plate she always was. She told me once that in their business, she could never go into the funeral home in jeans or casual attire. That would not be for me. I wonder if she ever got her hands in the dirt like I loved to do? After a kiss on the cheek, she immediately handed me the number of her cleaning lady.

"Her name is Nora Newstead," she revealed. "I told her you'd be calling. I have to tell you that when I mentioned where you lived, she hesitated. She knows the place to be haunted." She snickered with her hand to her mouth.

"Oh, for heaven's sake," I was now feeling disappointed. "What did you tell her?"

"What could I say?" Nancy was grinning. "I played dumb and said she'd have to take that up with you." She giggled again. "It is, isn't it, Anne?"

"It's not haunted. It just has the occasional presence of Albert's mistress, who is my grandmother. She isn't mean or scary. She's family, if you know what I mean."

"Tell that to Miss Nora! I can't guarantee she'll say yes, but she may try it as a favor to me. Let's just hope your little grandma will like her."

"Oh Nancy, stop it," I nudged her with my menu.

"Hello, ladies," said a man's voice from behind me. It was Ted.

"Ted, good to see you," I politely responded.

"Nancy, remember me?" Ted asked, taking her hand. "Ted Collins, Anne's old flame."

"Of course, Ted. It's been a long time," she said with a big smile.

"It's good to have you and Richard back in the community," Ted said, putting his hand on her shoulder. "What do you think of this brave married lady here?"

"She's done well, I'd say," Nancy said with a grin. I wasn't grinning.

"What makes me so brave, Ted?" I now put him on the spot.

"I guess I meant all the unknowns you've taken on with Sam and that big house on the hill," he said half teasingly. "Don't get me wrong. If anyone can pull this off, it's you, Anne." The tension was growing and Nancy knew she had to do or say something.

"Just don't worry about me, Mr. Collins. I think you have plenty to worry about yourself," I said mean spirited. "Are you ready to order, Nancy?"

"Nice to see you both," Ted said, grinning as he walked away.

"Holy cow," said Nancy, looking down at her menu. "I had no idea he took this all so poorly! He is still very angry. Did you know that?"

"Not really," I was now drinking some water. "He was so sweet when my Aunt Marie died. I thought he had moved on. He has a girlfriend, for heaven's sake. What is his problem?"

"You really don't know what his problem is, Anne?" Nancy asked, looking me straight in the eye. "He is still in love with you and he is just now going through the anger stage. He can't stand to see you so happy."

I responded by not responding and giving the waiter my order.

CHAPTER 43

W ork was piling up at the shop. This married life was taking me away from the shop more than I expected. There was a message from Mother to call home right away, but I first wanted to call Nora before one more day would go by without a cleaning lady. When she answered, I couldn't make out what age she might be, for I hadn't bothered to ask Nancy. She sounded younger than I thought.

"Yes, Mrs. Dickson, Nancy said you would be calling." she said politely. "I would have to see your home before I could commit."

"Of course, Nora, and please call me Anne," I stated. "How soon can you meet me at the house?"

"I suppose I could stop by around four this evening after I leave my job at the Prinster house."

"That would be perfect," I said anxiously. "I'll leave my shop a little early. Do you know where it is?" Of course, I knew the answer.

"I sure do, but I never drove up the hill," she explained.

"Great, I'll see you then," I confirmed, feeling a sense of accomplishment.

I knew I was going to have to keep any of Grandmother's activities a secret from her or she would fly out the door. I asked Abbey to stay until five so I could leave early. There were boxes and boxes to be checked in. With all the busywork, Abbey had little chance to experiment with any designing. I then returned a call to Eloise Marten, who insisted I was the only one she could talk to when she placed any kind of order. She was rich, lonely, and needed attention. As long as I gave her time to talk about all her family, she was sure to place a healthy order.

Mother was now calling on my cell phone, so I answered, carefully watching my clock.

"Hi, Mother. What can I do for you?" I asked.

"Amanda called and Mary is barely hanging on," she said in a shaky voice. "Julia is picking me up shortly to go see her. Julia called Ken, but I don't think he'll make the trip, knowing she may pass soon."

"I'm so sorry, Mother," I said, feeling so bad for her. "I'm glad you are going. I just can't leave right now or I would go with you as well."

"William and Amanda are by her side and they are so upset," she described.

"I'm so glad they have a little bit of a family to help support them right now."

"Julia is parking out front, so I have to go."

"Be careful and call me when you get back," I instructed. "Give her a kiss from me." I hung up, remembering the tremendous sadness when Mother, Aunt Julia, and Uncle Ken lost their other sister, Marie. A generation was leaving. Thank goodness Mother's health was hanging in there. Uncle Ken never complained, according to Sue, his daughter, so we should be thankful.

"Come on in, Nora," I said, greeting her. "I don't suppose we ever met before, have we?"

"No ma'am," she said in a soft voice. "I've been in your shop, of course. You do such pretty flowers there and all. Wow! This is a big house and a beautiful one at that!" Her eyes were taking it all in.

"We...Sam and I love it here," I explained with joy to make her feel more comfortable. "We did a lot of renovation, of course, because it sat empty for so long. The Taylors lived here. Did you know any of the family? Did you grow up here in Colebridge?"

"Not really," she shyly said. "My husband and I have been here about ten years, but we're really from across the river. I always wondered what was up here. You can't see much of the house from the street. You have such beautiful gardens, too. That gazebo out front is so wonderful. I always wanted one of those."

"I gave that to my husband at a surprise birthday party last summer," I explained, quite pleased with myself. "I was so afraid he wouldn't like it, but he did! Now, let me give you a tour and what might all have to be done in each room so you can be thinking about how much time you would need."

"Mrs. Dickson, I mean Anne," she said, standing still, "I hate to ask you this, but I have always heard this place is mighty haunted and I just don't think I could handle it if it is. Is that true?"

"We're living with a very old wives' tale that's been told over and over to where everyone wants to believe it. There's nothing here that scares Sam and me, and if there is, he or she is happy we're here. I feel so much love in this place, Nora. I hope that you'll find it the same. I've been researching the Taylor family and have found some things from them out in the potting shed. See the vase on the mantle?" We walked into the living room. "I found this all wrapped up in a really old quilt in the potting shed."

"Oh, my gosh. I love quilts. Was it a neat one?"

"It was at one time! I'll tell you more about that quilt later. Do you have any children?"

"No, but I had a stillborn two years ago," she sounded very sad.

"Oh Nora, I'm so sorry," I responded, shaking my head.

"We still have hope before I start my change of life, if you know what I mean." She was now blushing. "Do you and Mr. Dickson plan to have any little ones?"

"Not any time real soon, that's for sure." I was now taking her up the stairs. "We just got married and I have a flower shop to run. You'll find that Sam and I never go in some of these rooms that you'll clean, but they do get dusty. I am still furnishing some of them."

We covered each room. Nora was overwhelmed and admitted she had never been in any other finer homes than the Barristers' and ours. She said she told Nancy she would never clean at the funeral home. She also cleaned her mother-in-law's house on occasion. I could tell she was becoming less intimidated as we talked. I asked her to share a cup of tea with me, but she said she needed to go home. I told her that when the snow was completely gone I would give her a tour of my potting shed and the rest of the grounds. Also, she was very thrilled with my suggested rate per hour.

"I guess I could try it for a spell," she agreed, as we went out onto the porch.

"Oh, I would really be pleased," I said, softly clapping my hands. "So will Sam. He's been nice enough not to complain. I'll be decorating for Christmas soon and I want a great big live tree for that entry hall. What do you think?"

"It would be a sight, for sure," she said with a big smile. "If you need help with that, my husband is an outdoor person that could probably be helpful."

"Terrific." I walked her to her green pickup truck. "Here is my business card with all our information. So, do you think you could start this Monday?"

"Sure." She was smiling as she got into her truck.

I waved good-bye and went into the house to warm up. I turned on the fireplace in the study and went to get a glass of merlot. I felt another rock had been lifted off of me. I grabbed a piece of cheese and went back into the study to turn on the news. I couldn't wait to tell Sam the news of Nora.

CHAPTER 44

As I relaxed, my thoughts went back to Mother and Aunt Julia going to see Aunt Mary. Was I selfish to stay and accomplish this task or should I have gone with them? I then wondered how my husband was feeling and was about to call and check on him when the house phone rang.

"Anne, it's me," Mother said so quietly I couldn't hear her. "Julia and I are just now leaving Mary and I have bad news."

"Aunt Mary's gone?" I asked, already knowing the answer. "When?"

"She was already gone when we got here, sorry to say," Mother replied, holding back her tears. "They had not taken her from the room, so we joined Amanda and William, who were shocked in grief and needed our love and support, as you can imagine. They took it quite hard, so we decided to stay with them for a while. They knew the time would be coming and they did think about what some of the arrangements would be. It really helped them to talk the plans out with us. I've already talked to Ken, and he's flying in, however, Joyce won't be able to make it. She is having a small health procedure done and doesn't want to change her plans."

"I don't know what to say, Mother. You should be home in less than an hour, so do you want me to come over?"

"No, it isn't necessary," she said, sounding calmer. "It's been helpful to have Julia here with me. The service will be this weekend. Will Sam be home by then?"

"Yes, of course. We'll be sure to go and Sue will likely come with Uncle Ken. I'll find the funeral home and send a really nice floral arrangement. Was there a charity preference?"

"I will have to ask Amanda. I'm not sure. Thanks for taking care of the flowers. I'll call you tomorrow with more details."

"I feel badly now for not coming with you."

"Anne, Anne. If it were not for you and Amanda, we would not have found Mary, so you have done more than enough." She was now comforting me.

After hanging up, I just sat and stared. It was less than a year ago that we all just discovered the adopted daughter that our grandmother had given up. Grandmother had just lost another daughter now, a special daughter she had given up because her lover Albert Taylor would not acknowledge her or her pregnancy.

I wondered how our grandmother's spirit would react. At least I felt at peace that we all had taken in her existence as well her children, Amanda and William. I was glad the two of them had each other.

I was then jarred into reality when I heard my cell phone ringing in the kitchen. It was Sam. His timing couldn't have been better. I walked back into the den to tell him of the latest news. I could now feel my emotions breaking down into tears as I remembered what we had gone through losing my Aunt Marie. Sam was his comforting and loving self as he listened. His comforting words were always just enough for me to gain some perspective. I was glad he was coming home tomorrow. The big news of my day in employing a cleaning lady had just gone out the door. It was unimportant and it could wait.

I walked into the kitchen to put away my cheese and half-full glass of merlot, when I looked over to the center of the kitchen table. My constant ever-blooming lilies were now totally dead and hanging side to side from the vase. This was indeed a sign from Grandmother. She was now in mourning and I didn't blame her. I sat down near the vase and cried with her. No words needed to be spoken.

CHAPTER 45

Amanda and William quickly arranged the funeral details in one day. I told the girls at the shop of my plans for the next day and they were more than happy to keep things going. Sally had indeed taken over in management in every way except a title. I made a note to do just that very soon and give her a raise as well. Right now, taking a salary for me was unjustified. Abbey was now up to three days a week, which was not intended when I hired her. There were times I knew she felt like the oddball, but all and all, I had a good team in place.

Sam arrived home in time that morning to drop off his luggage and get in the car to go with me to Aunt Mary's funeral. We had time on the drive over to catch up on his trip and I shared the news of our new cleaning lady, Nora Newstead. He seemed pleased that it was arranged. I didn't want to ask about the timeline of Uncle Jim's job with

Martingale and decided to wait and let him be the one to bring up the topic.

A small crowd was gathered at the funeral home's chapel. Everyone was already seated. Aunt Julia brought Mother and Sarah. Uncle Ken came with Sue. Amanda and William were sitting in the front row trying to be strong. When the organ stopped playing, a handsome young chaplain appeared to greet us. I never asked, but was getting the impression that Aunt Mary did not have a church affiliation that was represented. Amanda then stood and addressed those in attendance, taking a deep breath.

"William and I are very pleased that you all took the time today to honor our dear mother, Mary Elizabeth Anderson. She was a terrific mother as she struggled with the unknowns of her own family. In the last year, we found that family, and it completed my mother's life. She was the happiest we had ever seen her. We talked about her failing health, but that did not spoil her joy for what was left of her life. When she drifted in and out of consciousness these last days, she spoke of seeing her mother and father waiting for her. God bless her soul." I shivered at the thought. "Please join us in the reception room on the lower level of this building for a light lunch."

Then to my surprise, Ken, her brother, came to the front and said a few words. "Our half sister, Mary, was a late surprise in our lives. When we all found each other, it not only completed her life but ours as well. We fell in love with William and Amanda, as if they were always in our family. Mary had to raise them after her husband died many years ago. I'm told she took in sewing when the children were little and then went to work for the Linden Linen Factory, working herself into a management position until her health failed her in recent years. We are all grateful that we were able to share what time we had with her."

By now, Mother and Aunt Julia were in tears holding onto each other. I looked into Sam's eyes and he knew how emotional this experience was for all of us. The chaplain's ending message was that life is so short and that we should make every day count. Man's weaknesses and the world's challenges are always trying to test our strength and faith, which we sometimes cannot control. I couldn't help but think of Steve and his sister. A series of life's circumstances had taken their lives way too soon. Aunt Mary, at least, was able to raise her children to adulthood and then thankfully discovered the missing link to her early life before she died.

Amanda and William were going to have her body cremated later that day.

The reception was memorable and short. At the lunch, we were able to meet some very pleasant folks that Aunt Mary had known in her life.

"I know many of these flowers came from your lovely shop, Anne," said Amanda. "A very large bouquet arrived without any card. Would you take a minute before you leave to see if you might remember who sent them?"

"I know they all didn't come from my shop," I said with some hesitation.

I followed her back up the stairs into the parlor where Aunt Mary's body lay in a closed casket. When she showed me the gorgeous floral display that was entirely white lilies and green ivy, I gasped, taking in a deep breath.

"Isn't this arrangement just amazingly beautiful?" bragged Amanda. "Do you recognize this from your shop?" I didn't know just what to say and how to say it.

"If I told you who this was from, would you promise not to ask any questions and accept my answer in good faith?" I asked, tearing up.

"You know?" She was puzzled by my reaction.

"Yes, I do," I nodded my head slowly. "These are from your mother's mother...Grandmother Davis. Lilies are her signature. Someday I will describe more in detail. Grandmother has not moved on. We'll see, however, now that the child she released for adoption has joined her." Amanda looked like she had seen a ghost. "Please be comforted by this token of affection and try not to figure it all out."

"Oh Anne, are you sure?" Amanda put her hands to her mouth in disbelief.

I smiled at her, taking her by the hand to join the others. Sam saw me coming down the stairs. He had been wondering where I had been.

"I'm ready to go, Sam. Things are good here," I stated as I gave him a kiss on the cheek.

Amanda looked affectionately at Sam and hugged him as she thanked him for coming. We said good-bye to the others and left hand in hand to go back to our lives in Colebridge.

CHAPTER 46

I was in the middle of examining my payroll the next day when I got a call from Sam asking if I happened to be free for lunch. He didn't sound like himself.

"Sure, if we can put it off to one o'clock when Sally returns from lunch," I replied, as I thought the day through. "Is everything okay?"

"The day could be better, but I'll explain later," he curtly answered.

"How about Charley's at one?"

"Thanks, sweetie." I heard the click of the receiver.

I had a gut feeling this had to do with him having to lay off Uncle Jim, but wasn't sure. I hated the thought of stress getting to him. It was hard for me to concentrate as I turned back to my payroll. I then heard Nancy's voice enter the front of the shop.

"I'd like to see the boss of this fancy flower shop,"

Nancy joked.

"Come on back," I called out to her. "I'm not accomplishing much here anyway."

"Looks like another snow shower is coming in," she announced, sitting down next to my desk. "It looks like we may have an early winter."

"That's actually a good thing for selling Christmas products if you can believe it! As long as the weather stays nice, they really don't get the Christmas spirit."

"That's one good thing about our business. There is no season, I don't think."

"Nancy, I bet you're wrong there," I challenged her. "I bet if you ask Richard that question, he'd have statistics that prove otherwise."

"Interesting. I'll report back to you on that." Nancy gave me a smile. "Now, the real reason I stopped by is to tell you that I called your mother this morning to see if we could have a work session on some of the baby quilts. I am down to just one of them, and Sue hasn't had time to work on them lately. I think her father stayed a couple of days longer when he came for the funeral and it set her back."

"Yes, he did. It was nice of him to do that and help Sue with a few things. He spent more time with William and Amanda too, making sure they didn't need some help with Aunt Mary's estate. He does some of that with his business. So what did the two of you come up with?"

"Well, Sue can come Sunday afternoon if she can bring Mia, which of course is no problem. Your mother was going to call your Aunt Julia, so if she makes it, we'll have a nice group to accomplish something. Will it work for you?"

"It should be no problem, from what I can see at this

time," I hesitated, now thinking about Sam's stress.

"These funeral quilts are so well received, especially when I tell them they are locally made by ladies in the community instead of some foreign manufacturer. Most of the parents want to keep the quilt, but I've had two families that chose to use them for the burial. Both of these were preemies and they didn't even own a baby quilt. I'm a bit more concerned about not being able to put my hands on our funeral quilt. You know, the one with signatures? I have a few staff people to ask before I panic, but I've always kept it in the same drawer. It's very bizarre!"

"Nancy, that's serious," I now gave her my entire attention. "I can see where a family member could think it would be a great memento to take from the funeral. People are weird the way they think they are entitled to things. I stopped lending props and stuff for events. Folks think they own them or deserve to own them because they have had to pay exorbitant flower fees!"

Nancy laughed as she shook her head in disgust.

"I've got to meet Sam at Charley's, so I'd better get on my way," I apologized as I got my coat. "Ask the girls if they want to join us. Sally is not a quilter, but Jean is quite accomplished at the skill."

"Okay I will, so be on your way!" she said as she walked me to the front of the store.

I found Sam talking to friends he knew when I walked into Charley's. He introduced me to a couple of them and then announced our table was waiting.

I got a simple kiss on the cheek before taking off my coat. I remained quiet until he felt like sharing his purpose. We placed a thoughtless order with a sweet young girl before

Sam got comfortable.

"I'm meeting with Jim tonight after work to warn him about tomorrow's announcement of layoffs," he divulged like a confession. I didn't respond.

"He knows through the grapevine that there are going to be some layoffs, but he has no clue he is one of them, trust me. That's how disconnected he's been from his job."

"Will he expect you to fix it?"

"Yes, unfortunately." He was looking down. "This is where he will lose it and turn on me. I know him too well. It'll be worse, however, if I don't share this with him ahead of time. Do you have any advice for me, boss lady?" Nice of him to respect my position as a boss, I thought to myself. Hmmm...

"There isn't going to be an easy way," I said, shaking my head. "I would be thinking about how you can help him after the fact. Do know anywhere he can apply or could you suggest he start his own business, like consulting?"

"Yeah, I thought of that but I can tell you that as much as I love that guy, I wouldn't ever go into business with him. If he goes there, he'll be even more upset with my reaction."

"I have a note on my desk that says, 'examine it, confront it, then let it go!'" I quoted. "It's really out of your hands after that. With your health concerns, you have to let it go, my dear, or it will control you. Do you hear?" He now broke into his first smile.

"This is why I love you so much, my wise Miss Annie," he said, kissing my hand.

"Not as much as that French dip you are about to bite into, right?"

We got through lunch with talk of Nora coming to clean, the quilters meeting on Sunday, and then finally the concern of where to find a great big live Christmas tree when the time was right. These were fun topics I no longer had to make decisions on alone. Was I letting up on my hold of independence? Hmmm...

Someone once told me that a strong, independent person will have the wisdom and strength to let go of things she knows others can manage better. I also learned there is a joy in sharing the choice of another person, especially of one she loves.

CHAPTER 47
🦋〰️🦋

S am was correct about Uncle Jim's reaction to losing his job. He seemed to think Sam should have done more to change their mind. What was making the situation worse was the rumor that Sam was to be promoted to vice president of sales and marketing, which was the stepping stone to becoming president of Martingale. Sam had not gotten the official word, but everyone thought it was likely to happen.

It wasn't long before Aunt Julia received the news directly from Uncle Jim. When she called to tell me, I was surprised she wasn't more sympathetic to his situation since it would be an adjustment to alimony and child support. Perhaps it was a little bit of revenge that guided her response. Sarah was taking the news much worse, according to Aunt Julia. I was then curious to see whether Aunt Julia would be joining us on Sunday afternoon at my mother's home.

On Sunday, Colebridge was like a beautiful winter glass

snow globe. The snow flurries were winding down and the sun was shining bright. Why did snow seem to clean and hide the worst of things? On the way to Mother's house, I made a small detour so I could drive by the snow-covered tree-lined graveyard where Albert Taylor enjoyed live lilies on his grave. The two inches of snow would be a good test of their durability. I had to get out of the car to make sure I was seeing the grave accurately. To my surprise, they were dead, turning brown, and leaning in one direction. The weather had never affected them before, so was it because of the death of his daughter, Mary? Was that why the lilies on my kitchen table had withered as well? What was the message Grandmother Davis was trying to send? I got out of the car and tromped in the snow, so I could take one of the lilies. I thought I would have it pressed or kept in something of hers when I returned home.

Arriving later than my usual time at Mother's, I was pleased to see all the cars, especially Aunt Julia's. When I opened the front door, a giggly, dark-headed toddler came right into my arms. Mia gave so much joy to all of us and she was growing up way too fast. The days were now history when she used to nap during our quilting in the basement.

I helped Mother carry mini cream puffs and pound cake downstairs. She was so intent on her mission that she did not grill me about why I was late. Nancy and Sue had already carried down the materials we would need to tie the quilts. Mother set up two tables, one to hold the materials and one to tie the dainty ribbons on the delicate quilts. While Mother poured tea and coffee, Nancy and Sue instructed us on who could do what.

"I want everyone to sign my quilt block before you go

home," requested Nancy. "These will all go into a friendship quilt when I have time, and you may all want to do the same sometime." We all looked at each other in amusement with the unexpected request. Leave it to Nancy to be creatively multitasking in her creativity.

"I wanted to know if you found the funeral parlor quilt, Nancy," I asked, getting even more attention from the others.

"What kind of goon would take a bloody funeral quilt?" asked Jean with a horrid look.

"I don't know if anyone really took it, but I can't find it anywhere," confessed Nancy. "I have asked everyone who works in the building and some don't even know what quilt I'm talking about. What's a goon, Jean?" We laughed.

"Oh, I'm sorry, Miss Nancy, I may have misspoke," she said, grinning. "A goon is a bad guy, I'd guess you'd all say."

"Well, I haven't panicked yet, but to my knowledge it has not left the building," Nancy explained. "We have seldom used it, and I have always put it back in the same drawer."

"Have you allowed anyone to put it in the actual casket?" I asked, trying to visualize where it had been.

"No, that would not be a good idea," she explained. "It has been on caskets and tables, but not in the caskets themselves."

"So, no chance of it being put in the casket accidentally when you were removing it from on top of the casket?" asked Mother, out of concern.

"I can't imagine that happening," Nancy answered with a frustrated tone.

"Who's the saint that the Catholics pray to when they lose something?" asked Aunt Julia.

"It's Saint Anthony, I believe," answered Mother. "It may be worth the trouble to ask, Nancy!" They all snickered and continued working.

"Well, I have some news to share for those of you who knew about the live lilies at on Albert Taylor's grave," I announced. "They are dead. How about that?" Silence fell in the room, as if I were going to explain why.

"Oh, what does it mean you think, Anne?" Mother asked.

Before I could answer, Jean and Nancy expressed their condolences again about Aunt Mary's death. I could immediately tell they knew there would be a connection.

"Think about it for a minute," I said before I took a sip of tea. "Grandmother is very sad. She just lost another child and the child's father was Albert Taylor. The lilies were a sign of her love for Albert; but now she has no one living who represents that love. It's over. It is sadly over. What do you all think?" They were all silently trying to digest the meaning of it all.

"That's a head scratcher," Jean responded. "Do you suppose your grandmother will take a fancy to stay away completely?"

"Something tells me that as long as I am living in Albert Taylor's house, I'll be reminded of her presence. There's no question she must be the ghost that so many have talked about in this town."

"I'm so surprised you aren't more frightened, Anne," said Sue, taking another cream puff in her mouth. "Oh, these are delicious."

"I got these at Nick's. Have you tried them, ladies?" I noticed I made Mother uncomfortable and she wanted to change the subject.

"I hope she behaves for my new cleaning lady," I said, trying to inject some humor. "I am so excited. I really, really need her! Some places in that house haven't been cleaned since I moved in."

"I think you'll like her, Anne," said Nancy, smiling. "She's a little homely, you might say, but she is scrubby Dutch and very dependable."

"I offered to help her, but you know Anne," Mother told the others. "I'm glad you're getting help, but it's a big house and it can't be cheap to get all that done."

"Well, I'm sure Sam can afford it now since he'll be getting a big promotion," Aunt Julia announced bluntly out of the blue.

"What's this?" asked Mother. All eyes were now on me.

"He hasn't received any promotion that I am aware of," I assured them. "Aunt Julia is correct in that it is a rumor at Martingale," I said with embarrassment.

"Oh, it's true and well deserved, I'm sure," Aunt Julia continued. "You may as well all know that Jim is out of a job because of the reorganization of the company, but that's not Sam's fault." No one knew what to say. It was a very uncomfortable subject for everyone.

"Oh, Julia, I am so sorry," said Mother, equally embarrassed. "I'm sure he'll find something. How long has he been with them?"

"Twelve years, I think," Aunt Julia's response reflected little remorse. "I wonder if Miss Brenda is losing her job," she curtly asked with a hateful tone.

"Who's Miss Brenda?" asked Jean, who was totally confused.

"I don't think we want to go there," I said gracefully. Jean took the hint right away.

"Well, Mia is really enjoying those books you brought

her, Jean," Sue said, trying to change the subject.

"She's been a good girl," added Mother. "If you ever need me to keep her, Sue, I'd love to."

"You're not going to take away my job," teased Aunt Julia. "Sarah would really be upset."

"Where is Sarah today?" I asked, now feeling more relaxed.

"She's with Jim," she answered. "They were going to take in a movie."

"Before you all rush off, I want to invite you over for Christmas Eve," Mother said, looking at me for approval. "That goes for you too, Nancy and Jean. You all have become like family, you know!"

"Oh, I think Mrs. Barrister would have a fit if I did that," Nancy teased.

"That is mighty nice of you, Miss Sylvia," answered Jean. "I will check with Al. We haven't chatted much about the holidays. Al and I have our Christmas on Christmas morning."

"What about you, Julia?" Mother asked.

"I think that can be arranged," she answered. "I don't know about Sarah just yet. Who knows what Jim may have planned for the holidays."

"Mia, Muffin, and I will be here," Sue said eagerly. "We will have our little Christmas in the morning as well. I'm so excited to have our first Christmas as a little family." It was great to see her so much happier.

Mother and I looked at each other in satisfaction. She knew I would be there as I had been every year of my life. It made her feel connected and gave her something to plan. I too was looking forward to my first Christmas with Sam. I had envisioned Christmas at 333 Lincoln the moment I set eyes on it.

CHAPTER 48

As the days became colder with morning frost, it was harder and harder to think about the walk up and down our drive each morning. I rolled reluctantly out of bed to begin my task, knowing the time was later than usual. I hated getting up in the dark. I noticed that Sam was still asleep, which was most unusual. I then recalled that he was very restless throughout the night. I put on my wool socks, knit running pants, and heavy sweatshirt before heading to the kitchen to put on the coffee. I pulled my red sock cap out of the closet, covered my unruly hair, and then put on my heavy jacket for a brisk walk. What a brave girl I was as I greeted the cold air!

There was just enough ice to have to hang onto tree limbs going down the hill. There wasn't much traffic, so I managed to walk on the road instead of icy patches along the roadside. Cars driving by were trying to intimidate me with their horns to tell me to get off the road. They were right. The brittle wind was burning my face but I kept thinking of the hot coffee waiting for me up the hill.

"Are you crazy?" That was the greeting from Sam when I opened the front door. "Do you know what the temperature is out there this morning?"

"Low, it would be very low," I teased, pulling off my outer garments.

"It is ten degrees with a wind chill that has to be awful," Sam said, pouring me a cup of coffee. "Drink this, you crazy wife! There's a fire on in the study. I'll be there shortly after this toast pops up." I began thawing out in front of the fire.

"I can't believe I was up before you, my love," I bragged as Sam joined me. "You didn't sleep well, did you?"

"No, it was a very long night," he said, shaking his head in disbelief. "I came down here for a while and turned on the TV to get my mind on something else."

"And what were you trying to not think about? This isn't like you. Are you feeling okay? Did you have those chest pains again?"

"I'm fine, but I was worried I would have them, I have to admit. I guess I'm feeling a lot of guilt right now and I feel like I've let down a good friend."

"What on earth are you feeling so guilty about?" I made him look me in the eye. "Uncle Jim did this to himself. It's not your fault."

"What I haven't shared with you is that I did get that promotion he was teasing me about," Sam confessed, looking down at the floor. "I am the new vice president of sales and marketing and was told in the same breath that Mr. Martingale will likely retire next year, which would surely make me president." I had to think for a moment about how I would respond.

"Oh my word, Sam! This is what you have been working for!" I stood up to embrace him. "Uncle Jim told me this would happen the night I first met you. He bragged about your dedication to the company. This is so wonderful, honey! What is wrong with this?"

"It's sort of like being careful what you ask for because you may get it! How can I feel good about this when my best friend has no job?"

"I see," I said, sitting back down next to him. "I think Uncle Jim is a bigger man than you give him credit for. I think he'll truly be happy for you."

We continued discussing the topic until the phone rang. I looked at the clock, knowing I was running way too late for my scheduled duties at the shop. It was Sally wanting an update and thinking that I may have had car trouble with the weather. I told her I'd be there within the hour.

"Speaking of promotions, Sam, I plan to tell Sally today that she is officially the manager of Brown's Botanical Flower Shop," I revealed, taking a big deep breath.

"Good for you, Anne. It's time. I bet most folks think she's already the manager since she's there full time. She's quite good and has been very loyal, from what you've told me."

"Yes, she has," I confirmed, now feeling more secure about my decision. "She could use a raise and I'm just darn lucky she hasn't gone somewhere else. I was going to take her to lunch today, but with this weather, I'm not sure we can work it out."

"Hurry on up to dress, Annie. I'm sorry I held you up," he said, giving me a hug. "I love you. I'm glad you understand why I'm struggling with this. I'll try to be happy about it all. Who knows, maybe we'll go out and celebrate the big raise that goes with all this!" I had never thought a moment about what that would mean. A raise at Brown's Botanical Flower Shop was non-existent. Sally would be the first to receive such a reward.

There was plenty to think about as I drove to work fighting the slow traffic. It gave me a chance to look at everyone's Christmas decorations downtown and up and down Main Street. There was nothing like the Christmas season in Colebridge. It came alive as every business was dressed up in its finest attire. Now that my shop was in full holiday trim, I would have to concentrate on 333 Lincoln.

Jean and Sally were busy in conversation when I arrived. There were calls to return, not to mention what might be waiting on my computer. The toasty warm shop had smells of coffee mixed in with the fresh roses sitting on the counter waiting to be arranged for the refrigerated case. My windows were frosted, which only added to the greenery and red bows. How lucky I felt in my beautiful garden, even in the dead of winter.

"Good morning, Miss Anne," Jean greeted. "It sure is a parky morning! I have a special bit of news to share, by golly."

"Is that right?" I eagerly responded. She had referred (more than once) about our floral refrigeration being parky, so I knew she meant it to mean very cold.

"When Al came home yesterday, he told me about a giant evergreen tree he found at some gent's farm he works with," Jean announced from the back room. "He told him he knew someone who was looking for a tree that big and the guy said for the right price, they could have it." I perked up at the thought.

"Well, I guess that's good news because I wouldn't know where to find one that tall," I confessed. "I've never seen one large enough in any tree lot. Did you get a name or address? I'd love to take a look."

"I did, Miss Anne," she chirped, as she happily shared the piece of paper. "I already told Al he may have to help put up the firry thing if you find one. He said he would. He thinks you're a mighty fine lady, Miss Anne." I took the paper note and put it in my purse. She knew she had pleased me very much.

"Jean, would you mind the front counter while I have a word with Sally for a moment?" I asked, taking Sally by surprise. Sally looked bewildered and didn't say a word as she joined me at my desk.

"Oh God, Anne, what in the world did I do?" she said in fear. I laughed.

"You have done a lot, my dear friend," I teased. "You have become indispensable here at the shop, especially since I married Sam. My role here has taken a different direction. As you know, I almost never have the time to help design or sell anymore. I feel bad about it at times, but it's where I am right now in life, which brings me to the subject of you! I want to officially make you the manager of Brown's Botanical Flower Shop." She looked totally shocked and somewhat speechless.

"Anne, good heavens," she responded in a big smile. "I'm honored, to say the least, but are you sure you really want to do this?"

"Holy cow, Sally, I have been thinking about this for at least a year," I confessed. "I'm just pleased you've hung in there with me. You are family. I promise to give you a nice raise, which I think we can afford. The shop has been doing well lately, thanks to you."

"Thanks so much, Anne. You know how much I love this place," she said, giving me a hug. "Jean is a hoot to work with and we get along so well. Abbey is learning quickly too, so we have a good staff for sure."

"I'm glad you see it the way I do," I said, feeling relieved. "I wanted to take you to lunch today to tell you but, as you can see, it's not going to be a good day to get away. Perhaps we can do it soon."

"Thanks again, Anne, and I'm glad you like Paige," she said, like she couldn't believe what was happening. She is making such a difference in my life. She is such a good friend to me."

"I know." I said reassuringly. "I'm happy for you."

We were interrupted by questions from the front counter and a busy phone that Jean could not keep pace with. It felt good to make the decision. I then thought about Sam who was having his first day as a vice president. What it would all mean would be very interesting.

CHAPTER 49

Jean was right about Al finding a perfect tree for us. Sam and I followed him out to his friend's farm and I spotted the tall cedar tree a good distance away. It was greener than most cedars around and it was nicely shaped. It was not as fat around as the others, but was tall and straight. Despite light flurries of snow, we got out and gave our approval for it to be cut down the next day. Sam wouldn't share what he had to pay for the great specimen, but he said I was worth it. He then teased I would have to accept less from Santa this year. I knew the thought of pleasing me made him happy.

When we returned home, we cleared plenty of space where the tree would be placed. It dawned on me that I didn't have one ornament to place on the tree and neither did Sam. We laughed and decided we got the cart before the horse. I told him I didn't care if it just had white lights. It was such a beautiful tree.

"I think I know how to solve this," said Sam as he went to pour us some wine in the kitchen. "We'll have a tree trimming party. We wanted to invite various folks over anyway, and we'll just tell them that to get in the door, they need to bring an ornament. When they see the size of this tree, they'll understand, believe me. What do you think?"

"I love it," I said as I explored the thought. "We'll do it on a Saturday night so I can prepare some refreshments during the day. Surely they'll have the tree up in a couple of days, right?"

"Sure," Sam agreed. "I told Al I would meet the guys here tomorrow afternoon to help them if they need it. Get on the phone and invite who you want."

"Please invite Uncle Jim. Or, do you want me to?" I asked, hoping it was a good idea.

"I'll do it," Sam volunteered. "I asked him to meet me for coffee in the morning anyway. I don't think Julia and Sarah would mind, do you?"

"No, I don't. It's Christmastime, for heaven's sake," I said, getting in the spirit.

The first person I called the next morning on my way to work was Mother. I knew it was my reassurance that I could pull off the party and knew she would love to help. I read her a list of people to call that we both knew. I asked her to include Amanda and Bill Anderson, but she quickly reminded me that they had gone out of town but would be joining us for Christmas Eve dinner. Mother thought it a grand idea to have a casual work party before all the traditional parties of the season would begin. She could sense my excitement with the thought of our first real party as man and wife.

The next morning, Kevin and I pulled in the parking lot at the same time behind the shop. He had a busy day so he arrived early. As we walked in the door, I told him about the party.

"Hey, you mind if I bring a date?" Kevin asked, shocking me completely.

"Wow, Kevin, when did this happen?" I asked, giving him a pleasing smile.

"Not long ago," he said with a bashful smile. "We've just gone out a couple of times, but I really like her. She's kind of different and really cute. Oh, she works at Pointer's Book Store. In fact, that's where I met her."

"Oh really? I wonder if she met my mother when she worked there part time?" I asked out of curiosity. "Yes, by all means bring her. Don't forget she has to bring an ornament too." He laughed in agreement.

"I doubt if she would have known your mother. I think she's pretty new there," Kevin added.

The phone reminded us that we were at work and it could mean money for the flower shop. It was Nancy.

"I was going to call you today!" I said cheerfully. "Can you and Richard come to our tree-trimming party Saturday night? You have to bring us an ornament because we have none. Did you hear me say *none*?"

She gladly accepted as she laughed and wanted to know the details. As we continued our conversation, she told me that the funeral parlor quilt was still missing.

"We finally decided to call the police," Nancy said sadly. "Can you believe it? Richard thinks I just misplaced it, but I'm telling you, Anne, I would never do that. Our staff seems to know nothing that is helpful."

"Okay, my dear," I said clearly, to get her attention. "I can't talk about it right now, but it's time you explore the realm of paranormal activity." I was trying to talk softly now so the others wouldn't hear. "I had to do it, still do, and probably will always have to do it."

"What are you getting at?" she asked, in the dark.

"You may have to think outside the box and consider case by case who used the quilt and what took place and when. For heaven's sakes, Nancy, you work in a funeral home! The spirits are running loose there with all sorts of drama their bodies left behind." Oh boy, I could tell I may have spoken too bluntly.

"Anne, do you know what you are saying?" she answered in shock.

"Yes, I do know what I'm saying. Do you want me to come over and play detective?"

"You always were weird!" she joked. "I guess I have nothing to lose, do I? You don't think that spooky grandmother of yours had anything to do with this, do you?" We both erupted into laughter.

"Probably not, but maybe she knows who did." I left her bewildered and we agreed to meet for lunch to discuss any possibilities, after I had accomplished some planning for the tree-trimming party.

CHAPTER 50

❧∨❧

"Oh, Sam, this is amazing and so beautiful," I said, walking in after work and hoping to see the tree standing. "It looks so much bigger now that it's in the house! Wow! It's almost touching the ceiling, isn't it? I hate the thought of having to put ornaments on it now." I had to giggle at the thought of this actually happening! "Yes, we'll put all white lights on it! The smell is just as I remembered growing up. We always had a cedar tree until pine trees came into vogue. Then Mother declared cedars old fashioned." I couldn't take my eyes off of this large living thing in our home.

"It was quite an ordeal, Annie," Sam complained with his hands on his hips. "The first stand Al brought to support it wasn't doing the job. Getting it in the door likely did some damage to the paint, so places will require some touch up. Al thinks we'll have to cut it up before it can leave the house. It has expanded since we brought it into the warm house. It will be a show, my dear! I'm glad you love it."

"I won't want it to leave here," I mused, as I went closer to the branches.

"There's quite a mess here with all the debris," complained Sam.

"I'll clean it up, gladly. It's the least I can do." I immediately went to get a broom and vacuum. "Wait until Mother sees this! Oh, and Mia will get so excited. Sam, this is the best Christmas present ever!"

He came over to my side, took the broom, and then kissed me with all his might. I knew it gave him pleasure to make me so happy. We both began the clean up and talked about how to arrange refreshments for the coming evening. Al told Sam he had left extra greenery from the tree on the side of the house in case I wanted to use it for more decorating. Sam took a break to pour us a glass of merlot, but I was too excited to drink or eat. I brought some red bows from the shop to place here and there with the extra branches of cedar, but I wanted the tree to be the focus.

The next day, Kevin stopped by to help me string the white lights. He continued to help in between his deliveries for the shop. When he got to the very top with the strand of lights, he wanted to know what I was putting at the top. He had the ladder and was in position, but I had no top. I had nothing and yet I had everything.

"Maybe someone will bring a top tomorrow night," I wished aloud. He snickered and then climbed down to gaze at it all.

"What should we cover the bottom with?" Kevin asked. "You can't leave this exposed."

I had to think. It would have to be something sizable. It

would be something that would wrap around the big tree base. Mother always laid white cotton and then placed her antique village scene around the bottom. I had nothing.

"One time, you brought a red and white quilt to the shop for a display. Do you still have that?" asked Kevin innocently.

"Yes! Good idea." I replied, going upstairs to look for it.

I opened the chest Nancy had given me where I had put the quilts that Aunt Marie wanted me to have when she died. They were mostly antique quilts except for one that she recently made. She said her mother had made some of them. Well if that happened to be the case, Grandmother Davis might have the perfect quilt for the job. There were four of them that Mother brought over after the funeral. The bottom one seemed to speak to me. It was red and faded green and looked like Christmas. It was quite worn, but the pieces remained intact. I made a mental note to ask Nancy what the name of the pattern might be. There was so much quilting—much more than we gave my floral quilt. I opened it up and was surprised to see how big it was. As I stared at it, I wondered whether Grandmother would want me to use it in this fashion. After all, water, cedar sap, and who knows what might get on the quilt. I brought it down to show Kevin and he took to it right away.

"This is perfect, Anne," he said with admiration. "You want something antique to go with this house. Even the tree is very old. Wouldn't it be neat to know just how old?"

We both got busy draping it around the base. Grandmother will strike me for sure if this is not the proper thing to do. It did look like it belonged there, though. The tree truly overpowered the entry room. Some folks may not even notice the quilt. Our stairway curved enough to outline the side of the tree, making one side available for easy decorating. It appeared to be customized to our liking.

I got up early Saturday morning. I called Nora to come by for a couple of hours to help me tidy up the place so I could make some trays of snacks. Mother was bringing some brisket sandwiches that were always a big hit. Aunt Julia and Sarah were going to make some Christmas sugar cookies and Nancy was going to bring cranberry and banana bread, which she made every Christmas. We would miss Uncle Jim's eggnog, but I certainly could not ask him to make it when I wasn't sure he would even come to the party. Most of the invitees commented they had never been to a trimming party, so the excitement was building.

It was just two hours before our first big party would begin. Sam got out of the shower and told me that he felt he had a good response from Uncle Jim when he asked him to come to our party. I was relieved and hoped Aunt Julia would be fine with it.

"Hey, they are both our friends," stated Sam. "They have to decide how they want to deal with it."

I was exhausted from all the preparation and sat on the bed to reflect on the evening. Did I think of everything? I hadn't even thought of what I would wear.

Should I be casual, as I knew most folks would be, or should I play the hostess with a more elegant look? It then dawned on me that I had never done anything like this before. Running this house was not like my shop, where I never second guessed my plans. Hmmm...

Sam saw me staring into space and came over to sit next to me.

"A penny for your thoughts!" he said softly as he put his

arm around me. "You have done a wonderful job, Anne. No one else would have thought of having that monstrous tree, I mean *beautiful* tree, but you! Everything you touch is special and you put so much love into everything. I am the luckiest guy in the world, you know."

I looked into his deep, dark eyes like I first did when we sat near each other at the dining room table just a year ago. He still turned on every light in my body. I loved him so much and reached to accept his embrace. We fell back on the counterpane quilt and melted into one. Right now, I didn't have to think what clothes to put on. I couldn't think of a better way to get the party started.

CHAPTER 51

I felt like a queen in her castle when I walked down the stairs as the elegant hostess of 333 Lincoln in black velvet slacks and a pure white silk blouse. It was adorned with my favorite pearls from Sam. I told the others to dress casually because, after all, they were to trim the tree. I was the hostess for the very first time, other than the Thanksgiving holiday. Our mothers, however, had dominated their presence over mine even though it was my house. I turned on some light Christmas music and lit some candles about the house that gave just the right ambiance.

Sam looked so handsome in his red sweater. He carried a grin from having the first present of the evening right in his own private bedroom.

Mother, of course, was the first to arrive. She used the excuse of having to get the sandwiches here in plenty of time. They did look divine and festive on her big silver platter. The dining room table would display all the delicious nibbles on my red tablecloth on loan from Mother. Sam was setting up the buffet with various wine choices and a bowl of his own concoction of spiked punch. There was a table by the tree where everyone could display their ornaments. Later, we would all place them on the tree together. Sam teased that as soon as everyone went out the door, I would be rearranging them in my own way. He knew me so well.

"This is the biggest and finest tree I've ever seen," said Richard as he and Nancy came in the door.

"Oh, Anne, how in the world did you get that in here?" asked Nancy in amazement.

I bragged about my elves and took her gorgeous ornaments to place on the prepared table.

Sally and Paige arrived the same time as Sue and Mia. Mia was half asleep until she saw the tree. She wriggled out of Sue's arms and ran around and around, pointing to the top. She didn't want to remove her coat in all the excitement. Sue finally bribed her with a cookie to accomplish the task. Kevin arrived with his date, Maggie. She was different, as he described. Her pinkish-red hair glowed. Her tattoos came alive on her bare arms in the dead of the winter season. She was terribly polite as Kevin introduced her around and he proudly bragged on how he and I had strung the lights. Abbey brought a girlfriend with her who seemed very pleasant. Two single friends of Sam's came that I had met once at Charley's. They were here from out of town so Sam invited them. I took coats, served drinks, and made cheery conversation knowing Aunt Julia, Sarah, Uncle Jim, Al, and Jean were still absent. I didn't want to start the trimming until all the guests arrived. In that next moment,

Sam opened the door for Jean and Al. They looked quite attractive together all dressed up.

"Here is something to wind things up a bit, as we say," said Jean, handing me a nice bouquet of mistletoe wrapped with a red ribbon bow. "A good kiss is better than getting snockered with plonk. I bet it'll hang quite nicely over that living room doorway. Oh yes, here's a silhouette ornament of our dear Jane Austen to put on your tree."

We bellowed with laughter at this delightful couple. I took the hostess gifts out of her hand and Sam took their coats. The ornament was hand painted and so pretty.

"Now, Jean, I know what getting snockered, is but what is *plonk*?" Sam asked, teasing her.

"Oh, some cheap wine," she laughingly explained. "Not that the distinguished Dickson's would have any cheap wine, of course." Little did she know one of our favorite merlots was always bargain priced at our IGA.

"Never mind the Miss," said Al with a smile. "I see the tree is still standing where I left it." He walked over with Sam to admire its stature.

Then the doorbell rang. I wondered if it was whom I had hoped for. To my surprise, in walked Aunt Julia, Sarah, and Uncle Jim all together! I couldn't believe my eyes!

"Hey, don't get excited here," Uncle Jim announced quickly. "These poor folks needed an escort for the evening and so I asked them if they would like a ride."

We laughed, giving them all a welcoming hug.

Aunt Julia was embarrassed and shaking her head in disbelief like she did so often around Uncle Jim.

"Oh, my goodness," screeched Sarah when she looked at the tree. "This is the coolest tree I have ever seen in my life.

Look at this, Mom!"

I watched Mother's reaction when the Baker family arrived together. She just grinned and shrugged her shoulders in wonder. Sam was now ringing our large dinner hand bell to get everyone's attention.

"Welcome to our home and Merry Christmas, everyone!" Sam shouted above the crowd, standing on the third stair next to the tree. "Anne and I want to thank you for joining us to christen our very first Christmas tree in our new home. Thanks to Anne, she chose well and I just hope she isn't thinking this is a Christmas tradition." Everyone laughed. "I want to thank Al Martin, who found the tree and used his amazing skills to help us bring the tree to 333 Lincoln." Al blushed with gratitude.

"Now I'd like to thank you for your generous ornaments to make this truly a special tree," I said, beaming with delight. "Please take your ornaments and place them wherever you like on the tree. We have a ladder standing by if you should want to use it." They all immediately hustled about the tree to find just the right spot for their ornaments. Uncle Jim took the ladder and said he wanted his snowman to be high enough for everyone to see. He bragged that Sarah had made it. He unfolded the ladder and others handed him ornaments as well. This was a Kodak moment for our Christmas album for sure. Mother already had camera in hand.

"Oh, what a beautiful tree topper," Uncle Jim announced down to me. "How in the world did you get that on there?"

I thought I misheard him in all the chatter.

"It is beautiful, Anne, where did you find that?" Mother said, looking up high.

I looked baffled at their remarks and went up a few stairs

to see what was on top of our tree. There it was. It was a beautiful white angel holding a bouquet of flowers. Then as I went higher, I noticed they were lilies. I looked down with a serious look to Mother. I didn't know if I was really seeing what I saw. Was someone like Aunt Julia playing a little joke on me?

"Mother, I didn't have a tree topper, not until this party began anyway." I answered, coming down to join her. I wanted to cry. Not here, not now, I thought.

"Well, I bet it was Sam who put it there to surprise you, don't you think?" she remarked, like she was talking to a little child.

I went to Aunt Julia in the dining room; she was about to bite into a brisket sandwich.

"Aunt Julia, was it you or Grandmother that put an angel on the top of our tree?" I asked, looking away from the crowd. She stopped chewing, remained silent, and walked to the door to see the tree from afar. She smiled back at me, shaking her head in wonder and amusement.

"Why does she love you so much, my dear Anne?" Aunt Julia said with a jealous tone. "She never does anything for me. I guess I should be glad she doesn't haunt the heck out of me with the way she always treated me. Besides, Anne, you live in her beloved Albert's house. She approves of you living here, so don't knock it."

With that, some singing started around the tree. I didn't know if I should cry or sing along with my tears. Will I ever get used to her presence? When no one was looking, I gazed to the treetop and whispered, "Merry Christmas to you too, Grandmother."

CHAPTER 52

The next business day, I resisted the thought of sleeping in, despite my exhaustion from the party. It was truly a success, which gave me energy for accomplishing more for the holiday. I had my full staff working today so I could have lunch with Nancy and then take in a bit of Christmas shopping.

When I arrived at the shop, Sally made it clear she had a headache from too much wine at the party and Abbey and Jean were busy chatting and working on a casket spray together. As I observed the staff, I was going to like having this bit of freedom with Sally in charge. I was missing out on so many events due to feeling guilty from being away from the shop. I told myself I would keep close tabs on my monthly profit and loss statement to make sure we could afford to keep Abbey on staff. She was working out nicely but she would be the first to go if I had to cut back.

Nancy called the shop as I was getting ready to leave.

She was running late and asked if I minded picking up something from the deli to eat in her office. I agreed, of course, but eating in a building where there were dead people would be a first for me.

I picked up some delicious smelling chicken Caesar wraps and parked by the side entrance of the funeral home where I had seen Nancy park before. I pressed the door buzzer and a young lady greeted me to take me to Nancy's office, as if she had been expecting me.

"Hey, girlfriend," Nancy greeted, "you don't mind eating a bite here, do you? I had Maureen bring us some lemonade. Will that do?"

"Oh sure. More time for shopping," I joked. I laid out the wraps as she poured the lemonade into our glasses full of ice.

"Anne, I thought maybe if we discussed the missing quilt here at the home, it might be helpful," she admitted with some embarrassment. "You said I should be thinking outside the box, and I honestly don't know where that is." We chuckled.

"I hate to talk with my mouth full, but I am so, so hungry," I admitted, taking another bite. "Did you make a list of all those families who used the quilt?"

"Sure, I did that shortly after it was missing. There are only about ten of them," she said. "One family wanted to use it yesterday. They had heard about the quilt and their mother was a quilter, so they thought it would be a nice touch. I told them it wasn't available."

Looking at her list, I said, "How many of these used the quilt inside the casket?"

"The quilt was never really inside any of the caskets that I recall. Most just wanted to use it for display with the flowers and memorabilia."

"Did you question those ten families to see if it could have been left in there when they closed the casket?" I queried, as I took another drink of lemonade. The taste made me wonder if Nancy had any clue about all my lemonade stories.

"Well, I questioned the staff, but I couldn't dare ask the families," she began, now becoming more animated. "I wouldn't want any of them to think we were accusing them of anything. Goodness knows, if the quilt had been left in the casket, it's too late now." We gave each other a funny look. Hmmm...

"Yes, but families get pretty emotional. If they liked what they saw, they could have intentionally taken the quilt home as a memento. Or, Nancy, they may think because it was used at the funeral, they could slip it inside as they said good-bye."

"Oh, our staff stays with them and we even have cameras recording during certain times in the room. We have a huge responsibility here keeping track of the deceased. We cannot afford for anything, absolutely anything, to go wrong."

"Well as you know, and you don't know everything, but I have had to deal with paranormal activity for the last year." She gave me a sarcastic look like I should "get real."

"You mean since you moved into your house?" She stopped from taking another bite. "I told you guys that folks said it was haunted."

"Well, it really all began when we started quilting Aunt Julia's quilt in my basement at home." I tried to act casual about the thought. "I don't want to go into it now, but what I have learned from it is that you have to address the paranormal activity up front and direct. I talk to Grandmother a lot. She is the source of my spiritual activity for sure. I am not afraid. She has never done anything to scare anyone." Nancy was silent like she could not believe what she was hearing. "For heaven's sake, Nancy, you are probably around many, many spirits all day long and you don't even know it."

"We just don't have things like that happen here," she quipped, becoming defensive. "That's just folklore and such. Funeral directors joke about it all the time, because that's what people always think."

"Okay, it's your business, but just take me to the room where the quilt went missing." She looked like she wasn't sure what to do next, so we finished our last bite of food and went down the hall to the storage room where I had been before.

"Grandmother dearest," I was talking aloud, "would you help us find the magnificent quilt that honors the dead here in Colebridge?" Nancy thought I was joking.

"Please Anne, don't make a joke out of this," she warned, giving me a hard look.

"Let's start here." I pointed to the drawer where Nancy last saw the quilt. "Open it."

Nancy opened the drawer and it was empty.

"You really thought it might just show up because you asked her?" She was now snickering at me.

"I have asked for her help before. She likes me more than anyone in the family for some reason. Aunt Julia said it's because I live in her lover's home." Nancy laughed and shook her heard in disbelief. "She keeps giving me gifts. By the way, where do you think that beautiful angel tree topper came from at the party? I had no treetop when the evening began, and no one took the ladder and put it there. It just happened to be an angel holding lilies. Lilies and lemonade are her trademarks."

"Oh my, oh my, oh my." Nancy was now sitting down. "Are you pulling my leg here?"

"I wouldn't do that, but what I am trying to tell you is that when you don't want to see things then they aren't seen. I'm not the only one who has seen her behavior." I was trying to sound convincing. "They are all just used to it now. There is nothing to be afraid of. I think it's comforting to the spirits that they are not ignored."

"I can't handle this, Anne. Let's get out in the fresh air," she pleaded as she moved toward the door. "I think my friend is losing her mind. It's time to shop."

Nancy took me by the hand, pushed a security button, and out the door we went. I knew I had gone too far but I wanted her to think about every option and even the supernatural possibilities. Shopping would indeed help smooth any fear I may have given her...or not?

CHAPTER 53

I couldn't believe how quickly the Christmas season was coming upon us. Everything seemed good. A brisk business and my first Christmas as Mrs. Dickson were as consuming as I had wanted it to be. I needed a new dress for the big Martingale holiday party that was approaching and I wanted to look fabulous. Unfortunately, the party would no longer include my Uncle Jim. Would his mistress, Brenda, be there?

I called Mother to see what I could bring for our traditional Christmas Eve dinner. She said she had it under control. The Carters next door came over last week to help her with the Christmas tree. She knew I had my own Christmas to plan, but it gave me a jolt of guilt and sadness. I had helped with our tree on Melrose Street all my life. I told her the table centerpiece would always be my treat and she was thrilled with that.

It was the morning of Christmas Eve and light snow flurries were a promise of a white Christmas. Sam was fussing in the kitchen, determined to make us blueberry pancakes. We were making traditions, wanting everything to be perfect for our first holiday as man and wife. Why did I feel everything was just a little too perfect? I poured my coffee and ventured out to the entry to see our big tree. It was still there in all its glory, proudly adorned with Grandmother's touch.

My mind wandered every direction on this sentimental day. I worried that I hadn't heard from Nancy since our lunch. They were staying in town to have Christmas with Richard's family. I probably said too much and scared her with ghostly thoughts. I told myself I would call her when I got to the shop to check on things. On Christmas Eve, there were always last minute orders for the holiday. I told Kevin to meet me there early to make sure we got out deliveries as soon as possible. I made a quick attempt at the delicious pancakes, kissed my sweet husband with my blueberry lips, and rushed out the door.

When Kevin arrived, I gave him his Christmas bonus. He was grateful and told me again how much he and his date had a good time at our party.

"I think we'll do a little New Year's lunch or something since we really didn't have our holiday toast here at the shop," I suggested, with good intentions.

"Hey, the party at your house took care of that, Anne," he politely responded. "I really appreciate this bonus more than you know. Wish Sam and your mother another Merry Christmas for me, okay?"

When he left the shop, I locked the door so I wouldn't

encourage any business I couldn't fulfill. We still had a few Christmas arrangements left in the cooler. In the past, I let the staff take home what they wanted.

I called Nancy and she sounded like she had just awakened.

"Merry Christmas, my dear friend," I greeted, sounding as cheerful as I could.

"The same to you and all your family, Anne! I was trying to decide when to call you today, so I'm glad you called."

"So, what are your plans?" She confirmed what she had told me before. "Has anything changed?"

"No, but Anne, I have to confess something that happened when I got back to my office after lunch."

"I think I know what you're going to say," I jumped in to say. "I went too far and I apologize. I wasn't any help at all regarding your situation."

"Not true, Anne! When I walked in my office, Maureen came rushing in to tell me that the funeral quilt was back! It was lying on the casket of one of our deceased in the blue room. At first, they thought I had put it there but it appeared when I was out with you. It was beautifully draped on top of Mrs. Taylor's casket. Maureen asked the others if they had instructions to put it there and they knew nothing about it. She said one of the family members came early and was quite pleased to see it, because Mrs. Taylor loved quilts. Maureen told them they shouldn't touch it until I returned. Richard agreed with them."

I remained silent until she finished.

"I ran immediately to the blue room to see for myself," she continued. "I had to admit, it was nicely displayed on the top of her casket with a spray of flowers that couldn't have been more beautiful. The spray came from your shop. I then remembered how Abbey and Jean were working on a similar arrangement when I stopped by. The really spooky part of it all, Anne, was that it already had the Taylor family name written in ink on the quilt just like the other families who used the quilt! How that could have happened without me, I can't explain. If I didn't have witnesses, I think I would be losing my mind right now. When I told Richard all about it at dinner, he advised me to forget it ever happened. That's the funeral industry for you. Anne, I know now it all had something to do with you requesting some help from the other side. This was strange and yet beautiful. Does that make any sense?"

How was I going to answer her? I didn't have answers.

"Oh, indeed it does. I'm so glad this had a good ending, but I have to admit that when you said the name of the deceased was a Taylor, it threw me for a loop. Taylor. I live in the Albert Taylor home, Nancy. My grandmother had an affair with Albert, remember? She's who I talked to in your office. Now, who this Taylor person is, I have no idea. There must be a connection, so I'll see what I can find from the floral order. This may be a far-out coincidence, but it's all too weird it was a deceased Taylor that ended up with the quilt."

"I was so embarrassed to call you, Anne. I wasn't taking you very seriously at all."

Now I felt responsible for making Nancy believe in things I couldn't even understand. Why didn't I just keep these strange occurrences to myself?

"In case this ever occurs again, you may want to think about what security you could put in place with the supernatural. I have no idea what that might be, unless your cameras can detect something. The actions and practices of this funeral quilt may create its own purpose, you know. You've made a special quilt that honors the deceased in Colebridge, not to mention all those darling baby quilts. You should be commended for that, Nancy. I'm so happy this is settled for the holiday. Now you and yours have a Merry Christmas!"

I hung up feeling I was beginning to be a part of two different worlds, thanks to Grandmother. I closed the shop and drove to my home to join my loving and understanding husband, Sam. For now, this discovery was going to remain something only Nancy, Grandmother, and I would share.

Did Grandmother borrow the casket quilt for another relative with the name of Taylor, or was this just another prank of hers? Hmmm...

CHAPTER 54

We looked like a couple on a Christmas card when we walked out of the door to go to Mother's home for dinner. Sam teased that, in the future, this would be our annual trip to Grandmother's house with all our little ones. I winced to myself, giving him only a smile in return.

Mother was delighted with the chosen centerpiece I brought. The place was still home and the smell of roasting turkey filled the house. When I walked into the living room, I saw the tree was not in front of the bay window and it was decorated in all blue and silver. What happened here since I left? Mother waited for my reaction.

"It was time for a change, my dear. I always wanted to go to something different like this," she admitted with excitement. "You have just inherited generations of lovely Christmas ornaments for that big tree of yours. Pick out what you want and throw out the others. It's a new chapter in the Brown family. Do you like it?"

"You are something!" I said in disbelief. I went over to hug her.

"This is very beautiful, Sylvia," praised Sam. "Thank you, my dear mother-in-law. You just saved me a bunch of money on that big tree of ours." We all laughed.

The other guests were arriving quickly and Mia was stealing the show. Sue had saved a new toy to introduce to her if she got fussy at the dinner table. She was turning into the best mother. It was fun to see Mia and Sue grow up together in their new role. William and Amanda arrived, bringing a fruitcake and a bottle of wine. Amanda shared that on Christmas Eve, ever since they could remember, they always sampled some fruitcake. Mother gladly received their gifts and told them they could carry on their tradition with all of us.

Aunt Julia and Sarah arrived in good spirits. I asked if everything went okay with Uncle Jim as their escort for the party and they said it did, dismissing the subject very quickly. Aunt Julia asked if I remembered one of Sam's friends at the party whose name was Harry. She thought him quite nice and noticed he was giving her enough attention that it led her to believe he may call or e-mail her. This was bound to happen. She was ready. I wasn't comfortable discussing the topic around Sarah.

Sam was now lighting the six candles placed on the table alongside of the centerpiece.

"Let us gather around to our place cards," Mother announced. "I've asked Sam to say the blessing, as he is now our man of the family." Everyone smiled as we connected our hands.

Sam began, "Dear Lord, this special night has brought us all together to celebrate family and the love we share together. Tomorrow, we celebrate your birth and pray that you would provide us with good health and happiness in the year ahead. Bless those family members who are not with us this day, as we pray in your name, Amen."

I felt pride as my eyes watered. Little did everyone know how important the words of "good health" meant for Sam and me. All were touched with his wonderful words. His leadership skills and ease of language showed up everywhere.

"As another male member of this great family, I would like to make the first toast to Sylvia Brown, my loving aunt, who has worked diligently to provide us a magnificent dinner," William announced.

"Hear ye, hear ye!" was said by all. This Kodak moment was no doubt one of the best ever!

The meal was welcomed as everyone overate. Aunt Julia's coconut cream pie and the after-dinner sherry made us continue the evening into the living room where we opened presents. Mia was "wound up tight" as her mother put it. She loved the pretty American Girl doll we had chosen for her. She was talking up a storm these days, and Sam was encouraging any little phrase or trick he could get out of her. I told myself I would never be able to compete with Sam if we ever had any children. There was something very sexy and attractive about a man and a child together, I thought as I watched him and Mia. Amanda took to Mother like another daughter and helped without behaving like she was a guest.

After the last gift was opened, Sam and I looked at each other, thinking the same thing. We wanted to leave, kick off our shoes, and snuggle in front of the fire in our own home. We gathered our things and did just that, with Mother's blessing.

CHAPTER 55

Driving up the 333 Lincoln driveway was a challenge. The light snow was turning into a thin sheet of ice as the temperatures continued to drop. We walked in to greet our larger-than-life Christmas tree, which we left lit while we were gone. Once again, it took our breath away! It didn't take us long to get in our robes and snuggle by the fire in the study. I decided to have some of Sam's leftover punch for my nightcap and Sam chose some English malt Scotch.

"Are you willing to wait for Santa to come in the morning, or would you like to cheat and open our gifts now?" he asked as he kissed my forehead.

"You already gave me that charming Jane Austen pin at Mother's," I kissed him back on his cheek. "It's darling and the other club members will be jealous! We have to wait until morning or Santa will not know our newly established routine at 333 Lincoln. We discussed the dinner and I briefly told him about Nancy and me talking earlier in the day and that she had found the quilt.

"Oh, very good." I realized he did not really know the whole story. "It sounds like she put a lot of work into that. Richard and I had a nice visit at the party. I like him!"

The full day got the best of us and our bedroom was calling its occupants. As we snuggled into the night, I think the sugarplums did dance in my head.

On Christmas morning, a light shone bright in our bedroom. I lay there for a second to recap the moment of the special day. I peered out the window, and the few inches of snow were just enough to create a glare as it covered the ground. Appetizing smells were making it up the stairs. Sam, the early riser, had started breakfast as usual. I knew it was bacon, but wasn't sure what else he might have to surprise me. I brushed my teeth, put on a red sweatshirt for the occasion, pulled my hair back, and crept down the stairs to join my husband.

"Merry Christmas, Mrs. Dickson!" Sam called out when he heard me.

"Merry Christmas to you, Mr. Dickson!" I responded with a kiss. "How can I be so hungry after that huge dinner last night?"

"You're just hungry for my love," he admitted. "I can put some in your waffles or my sweet embrace. Which would you like first?"

"I want that loving coffee!" I pushed him aside for the coffee pot. "Then I'll have some of that bacon. Waffles? Did I hear you say waffles? Yum! I haven't had waffles in ages." I didn't even know Sam owned a waffle iron. What else did I not know about this wonderful guy? Hmmm...

We ate at the kitchen table and tasted each other's syrup off our lips as we kissed in between bites. I felt the same excitement and anticipation as a kid on Christmas morning. Having Sam to share Christmas with was a whole new experience for sure!

"Can we just do nothing today and just play man and wife?" Sam teased.

"Sure, I was counting on it. When I was little, I'd stay in my pajamas all day and play with my toys." He laughed as he gave me a sexy grin.

"Speaking of toys, let's go see what Santa brought," I led him into the living room where we had a smaller tree by the fireplace. Sam turned on the gas logs and I settled down with his gift. He blushed like a little boy as he opened the beautiful package that I had gift wrapped for him at the store. The paper went flying until he found the monogrammed briefcase. Inside of it was the latest version of an iPad he loved so much. He was thrilled and was immediately focused on trying out his new gift.

"Hey, do I get a lump of coal or what?" I complained, waiting impatiently.

"You have to open this one first as a prelude to the real gift." He now handed me a beautiful red and white package.

Inside was a large coffee table book titled *Discovering Europe.* I wasn't quite sure what it meant until I opened another package of tour guide information and tickets to London, England! I didn't know quite what to say. This, I was not expecting.

"Are you serious, Sam? We are going to London?"

"London and more if you like," he was beaming at me. "We haven't had that honeymoon, Annie. I know how much you're enjoying Jean's stories and Jane Austen of course, so I thought this would be especially meaningful to you! Did I do okay?"

I wasn't sure what to say. "Is this affordable?" I knew it was the wrong question to ask. "Can you get away? Can I get away? Of course! This is bloody awesome, as Jean would say!"

"All bloody good then for a wedding holiday. Right, Annie?"

The next hour, we shared our coffee over busy chatter and talked about our gifts. It didn't take long for Sam to set up his new toy.

Sam went into the kitchen and I decided to call Mother and wish her a Merry Christmas. She was up and still fussing over the mess from the night before. I started to tell her about my Christmas gift when I heard a loud crash in the kitchen.

I heard Sam's voice saying, "Anne! Anne!" I slammed down the phone without saying good-bye. I ran into the kitchen saying, "Sam, what in the world happened?"

Then I saw Sam on the floor holding his chest. Broken dishes were strewn about the floor. It was my worst nightmare.

"Call 911!" he whispered in pain. "I'm sorry, but this is the worst pain ever. Get my pills on the dresser."

I wanted to scream aloud, but my instincts told me the 911 call had to be first. I became frustrated with their preliminary questions over the phone. I watched Sam trying to be brave with his pain. This was the heart attack that I had prayed would never happen. I hung up the phone, yelling various words of instruction as I ran up to get his pills. I almost fell down the stairs in my madness but quickly gave him a pill in hopes it would help subside whatever was going on.

"Relax, honey, and take a slow, deep breath," I encouraged, trying not to cry and instead show strength and courage in the situation. "I love you. Try not to think of anything. They will be here any minute."

"Get me a shirt," he instructed, still in a whisper.

"You won't need that in the ambulance; they'll cover you up." I was about to lose my mind. Please God, let them come soon and help him.

"I'm sorry, Anne, I didn't mean to spoil our Christmas!" He was now trying to sit up.

"Stop that and don't talk or move," I ordered, leaning him backwards. "I think I hear them. I'm going to let them in the door. Stay still and breathe. Breathe!" I ran and opened the door to a cold brisk winter wind. "In here! He's in the kitchen!"

Two very calm and capable young men knew exactly what to do and what questions to ask. The phone was ringing like mad. I knew it was Mother trying to call back to see what was wrong.

"I want to go in the ambulance with him. Let me get my shoes and coat," I told the paramedics. Sam had on his slippers, which would do fine.

They covered him up and his eyes were frozen on me in fear. They took him away and I went to get my purse, shoes, and coat. Sam was not able to talk with the oxygen mask on his face. I got in the ambulance and prayed quietly as I kissed and held onto his hand.

I was helpless and Sam knew it. One of the young men said Sam would be fine but he was just saying words. When we arrived at the emergency room with sirens blaring, they wheeled him away and out of my sight. I thought I was going to drop to the floor. The next thing was answering questions from an elderly lady who was neither very pleasant nor understanding. I wanted to run and find where they took him. She firmly but politely instructed me to stay put. After she had all the information, I found a chair in the corner of the waiting room where I could call Mother.

"It's bad, Mother. Sam's had a heart attack, I'm sure," I blurted out as I broke into tears that turned into sobs. She said she would be right here. She was closer to the hospital than I was. I was nearly in hysterics when a nurse asked for a Mrs. Dickson.

"Mrs. Sam Dickson?" she said, so calmly. "Your husband said to come tell you that he is okay and not to worry. Mr. Dickson's doctor has been called so we'll know more soon. He's in good hands right now with Dr. Wesley, who is on duty tonight." I sat and stared as if someone had shot me and I could not respond. I wasn't even sure what she said.

"When can I go see him?" I asked impatiently.

"Very soon, but not just yet. I'll come and get you shortly," the nurse said.

Mother found me in the waiting room. When our faces met, we both broke into tears and hugged one another. Then a doctor approached me and introduced himself as Dr. Wesley.

"Mrs. Dickson, your husband's doctor is on his way," he said in a calm voice. "I'm afraid we are going to have to do surgery when he gets here. He likely has a blockage and we can't afford to wait. He may have another attack. We gave him a sedative, but if you'd like to see him before he goes in, then come with me."

I looked at Mother in horror with the understanding that I may not be able to ever see him again. I got up out of my chair and followed him down the hall into Sam's room. Sam was hooked up intravenously and a breathing mask covered his mouth. He did see me approach his side and I told myself to be brave. He hated when I cried.

"Hey, sweetie, I guess we have to get this fixed once and for all!" I said, with an unconvincing smile. I kissed his hand and then his cheek. "You're probably drowsy now, but I will be here waiting for you. I love you more than anything in the whole wide world. You'll be all brand new for the new year!" I was babbling and on the brink of screaming.

"I love you," he whispered softly. Then he was out. He went into an unknown world without me.

"Mrs. Dickson, you must leave now," a voice said from behind. Sam was now being wheeled away from me. I thought I was going to be sick and asked for a restroom.

When I found my way back to Mother in the waiting room, she was joined by Aunt Julia who was crying too. I stared at them both. They knew the pain and fear I was confronted with for the first time in my life. We engulfed in one big hug. I was shaking and crying in horror of the unknown.

"I can't lose him," I cried loudly. "I just found him!"

The Colebridge community continues!

What you can look forward to:

1. Will Sam survive his surgery?

2. Will the outcome of Sam's condition
affect Anne's future plans?

3. How does Jane Austen influence the quilters?

4. Will Brown's Botanical continue to thrive
or is there trouble ahead?

Cozy up with more quilting mysteries from Ann Hazelwood...

WINE COUNTRY QUILT SERIES

After quitting her boring editing job, aspiring writer Lily Rosenthal isn't sure what to do next. Her two biggest joys in life are collecting antique quilts and frequenting the area's beautiful wine country. The murder of a friend results in Lily acquiring the inventory of a local antique store. Murder, quilts, and vineyards serve as the inspiration as Lily embarks on a journey filled with laughs, loss, and red-and-white quilts.

THE DOOR COUNTY QUILT SERIES

Meet Claire Stewart, a new resident of Door County, Wisconsin. Claire is a watercolor quilt artist and joins a prestigious small quilting club when her best friend moves away. As she grows more comfortable after escaping a bad relationship, new ideas and surprises abound as friendships, quilting, and her love life all change for the better.